LOST MEMORIES

Julie Coffin

This Large Print book is published by BBC Audiobooks Ltd, Bath, England and by Thorndike Press®, Waterville, Maine, USA.

Published in 2005 in the U.K. by arrangement with the author.
Published in 2005 in the U.S. by arrangement with Julie Coffin.

U.K. Hardcover ISBN 1–4056–3162–7 (Chivers Large Print)
U.K. Softcover ISBN 1–4056–3163–5 (Camden Large Print)
U.S. Softcover ISBN 0–7862–7012–8 (Nightingale)

The text of this Large Print edition is unabridged.
Other aspects of the book may vary from the original edition.

Set in 16 pt. New Times Roman.

Printed in Great Britain on acid-free paper.

British Library Cataloguing in Publication Data available

Library of Congress Control Number: 2004114015

CHAPTER ONE

It was a strange feeling, a floating feeling. Detached. As if her body didn't belong to her. Or was it her head? She wasn't sure.

Reluctantly she opened her eyes but immediately bright sunshine seared them, making her shut them quickly and draw in her breath.

She had to look though. She had to know. But what was it she had to know? Once more she opened her eyes. This time cautiously and slowly, widening them gradually.

The opposite wall of the room was white, patterned with the silhouette of windows.

Her gaze moved on, past a part-open door, a washbasin with a mirror above and a low white cupboard. Her neck felt stiff as she turned it.

And then she realised what she should have known immediately. She was in a bed, each side railed with shining chrome, a sheet tucked around her so tightly it held her confined.

Just like a prisoner, she thought, and her body shuddered. But why? What am I doing here? Where am I?

And then a far more terrifying thought appeared from nowhere into her head. And I can't remember who I am!

She tugged frantically at the sheet,

loosening it, drawing her legs up to her chest to release them.

Then, carefully, she eased herself away from the restraining rails to the end of the bed and sat up.

Her feet met the coldness of the floor and, gripping the rail for support, she stood, shaking from the effort. The mirror! She had to reach the mirror.

Her limbs were like cotton wool and her head pounded. Each step felt like it was taking for ever. Now she was there. Her fingers gripped the cold edge of the basin, knuckles white.

A face stared wide-eyed back at her. An oval face framed by fair hair, long, stringy, and slightly uneven over her head.

The eyes she saw were grey, thickly fringed with dark lashes; the nose small; the mouth full-lipped and slightly curved as if once it had smiled quite a lot. But none of this was familiar. It was the face of a total stranger.

'What are you doing out of bed?'

The stern, male voice startled her and she spun round, losing her grip on the washbasin and almost falling.

An arm caught her round the waist and she leaned into his chest, her legs beginning to give way.

'You really shouldn't be up, you know.' His voice was a lot more gentle now. It was a warm voice, she decided. A voice that curled round her, protectively, like his arm.

'Where am I?' she asked.

She felt the line of his chin move against her forehead and heard his laugh.

'A reasonable question under the circumstances,' he said, guiding her back to the bed.

She watched his hand—a slender, long-fingered hand with well-shaped nails, she noticed—lower one of the side rails, heard the clang as it snapped down, and let herself sink back into the pillows.

The rail rattled back into place again and once more she felt trapped, caged like a prisoner.

Her body stiffened and she looked up at him in terror.

'It's OK,' he soothed, his fingertips lightly touching her cheek. 'Just a precaution to stop you falling out.'

'But I won't,' she protested, lifting her head to glare at him.

Amused grey-blue eyes smiled back at her from a long, rather narrow, bearded face and his mouth curved, sending tiny lines rippling out into the thick fairness of his hair. His smile began to annoy her.

'You haven't answered my question. Where is this place? What am I doing here? And who on earth are you?'

Instantly the humour vanished, leaving his face bleak and angular.

'You're in Trevellian House—a private hospital on the Lizard in Cornwall. And I'm Daniel Brett, the doctor in charge. As to what you're doing here . . . well, I was hoping you could tell me that.' His eyes searched hers. 'What's your name?'

She remembered the mirror and the face reflected there. It had to be her own. And yet, it was as though she'd never seen it before.

His gaze clouded at her silence and she saw his square forehead crease into a frown.

'So you don't want to tell me who you are?'

'I don't know who I am,' she retorted. 'All I know is that I'm here. I have no memory of anything else. I don't even recognise myself in the mirror.' Her mouth trembled.

'You've no brain damage,' he mused, almost as if speaking to himself. 'We put you through the scanner soon after you arrived. No injuries to your body either, apart from a few minor scratches. But that's to be expected.'

'Expected?' she queried, puzzled by his tone.

'You were found wandering along the cliff path above Housel Bay. A party of ramblers saw you. To be honest, they thought you were drunk or drugged.' His mouth was set in a grim line. 'We do get a few strange people around in the summer months. Anyway, the path's quite steep in places. Bordered with blackthorn, too. And it runs very close to the edge with a sheer drop to the rocks below. Trevellian House isn't far, so they brought you here.'

'But didn't I have anything to identify me? A bag? Things in my pockets?'

'You were completely naked.' One of his eyebrows twitched upwards. 'That's why the ramblers noticed you.'

'Naked?' She was conscious of a wave of colour blazing into her face.

'Not something you normally do,' he assured her quickly.

'I'm glad to hear it—how do you know?'

'Your suntan leaves the perfect outline of a bikini.'

'So what was I doing, wandering about like that? How did I get there? This is Cornwall, you say? Do I live here? Am I on holiday? Are there others? A family? Friends?'

Her voice rose hysterically, her hands clutching at the rails of the bed.

'Just relax. There's nothing to worry about.' She noticed his long, cool fingers encircle her wrist and sensed he was checking her pulse. 'You were in a state of shock when they brought you in.'

His gaze suddenly moved away from hers and grew intent. With a flinch, she felt the prick of a needle on her skin.

'In fact,' he continued smoothly, raising his eyes to meet her own again, 'I'd say it was more than shock. Petrified with fear is a better description. In my opinion, something, or someone, had terrified you.'

‘So what happens now?’ she asked, trying desperately to make herself focus on his tall, white-coated figure. His voice seemed to be coming from a long, long distance but his reply chilled her.

‘I’m keeping you here.’

Momentarily, she struggled to lift her head. The effort was too much. His thin, tanned face was blurring.

All she could see were those deep, grey-blue eyes fixed on her; she felt the clasp of his fingers round her wrist and heard the dull roar of the sea somewhere nearby.

Her lashes brushed her cheek and she breathed deeply.

There was a scent of lavender. Or it could have been cinnamon or spice. Or perhaps something like that.

Not flowers. Definitely not the sweet perfume of flowers, of that she was quite certain.

It was a pleasant smell though. A warm smell.

There was something comforting and soothing about it. Her mouth curved with pleasure.

* * *

The room was dark when she woke, although as she focused, she realised it was more dusky than dark. Somewhere a light shone, or perhaps it was the moon.

She turned her face reluctantly towards the window. It glowed with brightness, so it must be a security light, she decided. A place like this would need protection. A place like what, she asked herself. What is it like, this private hospital?

Trevellian House. From the style of window, it appeared to be old and yet the fittings inside the room were modern, reasonably new, in fact.

And Dr Brett is in charge, she recalled, even though he seems very young. In his thirties, maybe.

So who else is here? He must have staff—nurses, other doctors. And surely there were other patients.

And yet, everywhere seems so silent. She would have expected there to be noise. Hospitals aren't silent at night. Patients need attention whatever the hour of the day.

Unless . . . Her spine prickled. I can't be the only patient, she reasoned. There must be others. There must.

She listened, straining her ears for the slightest noise. If only she could hear footsteps, a door opening or closing . . . the rattle of a trolley. But there was nothing, just silence—total silence.

I am the only person here, she thought. I'm a prisoner—his prisoner. He's not a doctor!

Everything he's told me is a lie. A total lie. I

wasn't found on the cliff. He's kidnapped me.

Fear sliced into her, catching at her breath, making her heart pound until it threatened to choke her.

She knew at that moment she had to get away from here. Her head swam as she stood up and she caught at the metal bed-rail, waiting until the room settled down around her.

The window. She had to reach the window. If she could do that, she could escape. Step by step, she moved across the room, pausing every so often to allow her legs to become steady.

Her fingers caught the windowsill, then travelled up the glass to discover sash windows. Cautiously, she began to push one upwards. It moved about ten centimetres, then stopped. No matter how hard she tried it wouldn't budge any farther.

And then the wailing began.

*　　*　　*

The noise erupted around her so suddenly that she couldn't believe it, a cacophony of sound reverberating. Her fingers froze on the window frame.

Light blazed into the room, flooding every corner of the darkness. And when she turned her head, Dr Brett stood there, filling the doorway with his height, his angular face taut.

'I should've guessed.' He sighed. 'What are you trying to do this time?'

'Escape,' she said defiantly. 'You can't keep me here.'

His arm slipped firmly round her shoulders and her body went rigid.

'I can and I am,' he replied. 'Now get back into bed while I switch off that alarm. Then we'll talk.'

'What is there to talk about?' she retorted. 'I've told you—I'm no-one. I know nothing. Everything's a total blank.'

'Just get into bed,' he said, lowering the rail once more. 'Come on. No arguments. This noise will drive everyone insane if I don't stop it soon.'

Reluctantly, she obeyed, sliding down into the warmth of the covers, letting her head sink back into the pillow, closing her eyes. That same spicy smell lingered after Dr Brett had left the room.

I am a prisoner, she thought. I can't even move without him knowing. A cotton-wool muzziness clouded her brain making it difficult even to think. I have to remember. There must be some clue. I can't just be nobody. Someone must know who I am.

She stretched out her hands and studied them. They were suntanned and well-kept with neatly-shaped nails. Light scratches criss-crossed the skin.

The cliff path is bordered by blackthorn

bushes, Daniel Brett had told her. Maybe that was how she got these scratches. The shriek of the alarm ceased, leaving a hollow silence.

Her ears were still ringing with the sound when Dr Brett walked back into the room.

She hadn't heard his footsteps and, glancing down, she saw the deep rubber soles of his shoes. No wonder he can move so silently, she thought, and her spine prickled again.

'Now,' he said, resting his hands on the rail of the bed. 'Why don't you tell me what's troubling you?'

'What's troubling me?' she burst out. 'Isn't that a bit of a thoughtless remark to make? I wake up, find myself trapped here and you ask what's troubling me.'

'You're not trapped,' he said mildly.

'Aren't I?' she demanded. 'You try lying here, behind bars, drugged by some unknown injection, with alarms sounding every time you move, and you might have the same impression.'

She watched his fingers tighten round the chrome bars.

'It's not like that.'

'Convince me,' she snapped.

'You were in a hysterical state on the cliffs. Until I know the reason for that, you need sedating. Look at you now—the slightest thing triggers you off. You're a danger to yourself. And as for the alarm, that's to prevent intruders getting in. Every window is secured in that way. It's quite a vulnerable spot here on the coast.'

'Is it? I wouldn't know, would I? You're forgetting I have no idea what's outside the four walls of this room.' Sarcasm laced her words.

'In the morning everything will be quite different,' he said gently. 'Now go back to sleep.'

She glowered up at him.

'No more surreptitious injections to make me?'

He gave a wry smile.

'I'm sorry. I should've warned you about that, but at the time you were distressed enough. And you'd never have agreed if I'd asked you first, would you?'

'I should still have been given the choice.'

'Ethically, yes, but sometimes a doctor has to decide what's best for a patient.'

'And you are a doctor?'

His dark brows drew together in a frown.

'Do you doubt it?'

'I only have your word.'

'You think I'd go to all this trouble to abduct you?' His mouth tilted with amusement.

'People do strange things,' she replied defensively.

'I don't.'

'How can I be sure of that?'

He leaned away from the bed and studied

her thoughtfully.

'Only by trusting me.'

'I wish I could.'

'Try.' Laughter returned to his voice. 'It's your only choice, isn't it?'

'That's what frightens me.'

The humour vanished and she saw his eyes widen in surprise. One hand reached down and touched the curve of her cheek. Instinctively, she turned her face away, letting his fingers slip on to the pillow.

'You really are frightened?' he questioned. 'Of me?' His voice sounded incredulous.

She nodded, refusing to meet his gaze.

'But why? What have I done?' he asked gently.

'You're keeping me here. Isn't that enough?'

'Only until I find out exactly what caused your amnesia. Something must have caused it. And as there's no sign of injury to your head, then it could be some form of shock—a blotting out of some incident you don't want to remember.'

'And will my memory ever come back?' she asked plaintively.

'Exceptional trauma can prevent it, but it has to be something pretty devastating, perhaps witnessing something terrible—a violent event, like murder for instance.'

'Murder?' She gasped. 'Witnessing it, or . . .' She hesitated, then continued in a rush of words. 'Actually carrying out that act?'

'I think we have to consider all possibilities.'

'So what you're saying is . . . I could have murdered someone and then blotted out the whole event as a form of defence.'

'I doubt it.' He smiled. 'You're not the type.'

'How do you know?' she demanded. 'Is there a particular type? Surely anyone can commit murder if provoked?' She eyed him through her lashes. 'Even you,' she said softly.

'My job is to preserve life, not extinguish it,' he said, his back stiffening.

'But you do have excellent ways and means at your disposal for committing the perfect murder, don't you?'

He raised his eyebrows and a smile curved his mouth again.

'You mean, like a lethal injection?'

'Like a lethal injection,' she agreed. 'After all, who'd know?'

'Yes,' he said. 'As you so rightly say, who'd know. But none of this solves your problem, does it? All we can assume is that you were on the cliff path. Whatever caused your amnesia happened in that vicinity.'

'But what about the fact I wasn't dressed? How do you explain that?'

He wrinkled his nose.

'Well, you could have been skinny dipping—swimming in the nude. Lots of people do. There are plenty of deserted little coves round this way.' He paused to look at her thoughtfully.

'Or you could have stripped off your clothes because they were soaking wet, or perhaps soaked with something else . . .'

CHAPTER TWO

'However,' Daniel Brett continued, 'that's all supposition, isn't it? My job now is to get you fit again.'

'I'm not ill,' she protested.

'Amnesia is a form of illness,' he said, 'and you should be trying to get some sleep just now.'

'What about you?' she asked, noticing that he was still dressed in a blue striped shirt and dark trousers under his open white coat.

Dr Brett gave an abrupt laugh and moved towards the door.

'Me? Oh, I never sleep,' he said, and was gone as silently as he'd come.

But she couldn't sleep.

Her mind was too active, delving deep, trying desperately to find some chink in the veil that hid everything from her. She must have some kind of memory, she thought.

Slipping out of bed once more, she went back to the mirror and stared at her image.

The wide, grey eyes looking at her were full of anguish.

It's not even a beautiful face, she decided forlornly. And as for the hair—it's so untidy and unkempt. I can't believe I would normally want to look like this. She frowned at herself.

She couldn't even think if this was the way it was supposed to be. Perhaps it was usually in a completely different style.

The effort made her head ache and she watched the reflected eyes swim with tears, blurring her vision. It's impossible, she raged. But someone somewhere must know. I can't just spring from nowhere. I have to have a past life.

Maybe things will seem more normal when I wake up tomorrow, she thought. Right now, I need to get some decent sleep.

In the morning everything will be different. That's what Daniel Brett said. He should know, shouldn't he? He is a doctor, after all. Doubt filtered into her mind once more. Or so he says, she thought.

She climbed back into bed, pulling the covers round her, suddenly exhausted.

In the distance she could hear sea crash against rock and the slow drag of shingle as it retreated. It was a soothing sound, repeating itself in a gentle rhythm.

Tomorrow . . . or is that today, she asked herself, she would be able to go out to see the sea for herself.

She yawned widely, aware of sleep starting to take over again. Her gaze moved to the window and she saw glimpses of pale sky in between the heavy, dark clouds.

Dawn was beginning to break and she found it hard to believe the events the previous day had brought. But this was a new day and maybe things would become a little clearer . . .

*   *   *

She was walking up a gravel path, the fine stones gritting under her thin, strappy sandals.

One stone caught between her toes and she bent to remove it, her blue denim skirt swirling over her feet.

The door ahead of her was open. She could see the polished wood of the hall gleam in the sunshine.

With the annoying bit of grit gone, she stood up again, sweeping back the thick mane of her hair from around her face with one hand, feeling it settle heavily on her shoulders.

There was a faint rustle of dry stems and from under one of the lavender bushes bordering the path stepped a tortoiseshell cat, tail curling upwards. It pressed its silky head against her bare skin, weaving its body round and round her ankles, preventing her walking farther.

'Toby, you old darling,' she breathed, stooping to stroke the warm fur. The sharp tang of lavender surrounded her with its fragrance.

* * *

'Your breakfast is getting cold.'

Daniel Brett's voice shattered her dream and she opened her eyes to see a tray on the bedside table.

'Toby,' she said, sitting up slowly. 'The cat's name is Toby.'

'What cat?' he asked.

She closed her eyes, her teeth biting down into her lower lip.

'It was orange and black and grey. Fluffy. It was under the lavender.'

Dr Brett smiled at her.

'You were dreaming,' he said.

She shook her head.

'It wasn't just a dream. How else would I know his name is Toby?'

'You could have made it up yourself,' he suggested.

'It's his name,' she insisted. 'I'm quite certain of that.'

He leaned over the side of the bed.

'Can you remember anything more?'

'There was a path. Gravel—and a door.' She wrinkled up her face in an effort to recall it. 'Painted black, I think,' she said. 'The walls on either side were whitewashed, and made of stone. And there was lavender. The path has lots of bushes on either side. You can't help brushing against them as you go by, they're so thick and straggly. And the smell is incredible. Beautiful.'

'Go on,' he prompted.

'I can't. That's it.' She glared up at him. 'If you hadn't woken me I'd have been inside the door and then . . .' Her voice trailed away.

'It was only a dream.'

'But so vivid,' she cried. 'Everything was clear. It must be somewhere I know—mustn't it?'

'Could be. Now, eat up. Someone from the police is coming to see you in half an hour.'

'Police?'

'I had to report what had happened,' Daniel said gently. 'Although I must admit they didn't seem too concerned about it. No-one has been reported missing, so there wasn't quite the same urgency, I suppose. With their agreement, I've arranged also for a man from the local newspaper to interview you later on today. A little publicity might help identify you.'

Without knowing why, she felt uneasy. It was the mention of the police. Her hand shook as she picked up the glass from the tray and sipped orange juice. Then she began to cut into a pile of scrambled egg.

'When did you eat last?' he asked. 'You're ravenous. Take it slowly. Would you like more toast?'

She nodded, her mouth too full to answer.

It was only when he'd left the room that the

thought occurred. Who had brought her food? Was it Daniel Brett?

Surely there must be nurses or auxiliaries, or someone? And yet the only person she'd seen all the time she'd been at Trevellian House was Dr Brett, no one else at all.

*   *   *

The police interview was very brief. In ten minutes, it was all over. All they'd been after were for routine questions to be filled in on a form. They asked for her name and address, date and place of birth. But they all received negative answers.

Dr Brett was questioned far more closely than she. But then, she reasoned, he does know the details. All I can remember is waking up here.

Shortly after, the reporter arrived—an older man whose age she couldn't define. With him came a smell of cigarette smoke. It seemed to permeate the whole of him, his clothes, hair and skin. She quite expected to see it trail from his mouth when he interviewed her.

And he did interview her very fully. More so than the police sergeant. Not that she could answer a great deal.

Dr Brett stayed in the room, and she wondered why. The replies she gave were no different from those she'd given earlier that morning. How could they be? She knew nothing.

'Found naked, you say?'

She watched the bloodshot eyes narrow.

'So I'm told,' she said.

'Out by Housel Bay?'

'Apparently so.' She nodded. 'But I've no idea where that is.'

'And naked.' He repeated the word and lingered on it, making her feel uncomfortable.

His pen was making notes, scurrying across the crumpled pages of a lined pad. She watched a jumble of scattered words appear, but couldn't read them.

'I'd need photos. D'you mind? I prefer to take my own—that way, I get what I want.'

He was unzipping a canvas bag as he spoke, and lifted out a small camera. The fact it was so small surprised her.

She'd imagined something much bigger, with a huge flashlight attached, like the ones you see in old films.

The very fact she could picture one made her stop and think. What on earth had made her think of one in the first place?

'Can you sit up? I'd like to get as much of you in the photograph as possible.'

The flash of the camera dazzled her, leaving pale moons of light floating in her vision.

Quickly, she closed her eyes but they remained, hovering like fireflies.

'I think that's quite enough.'

She was glad to hear Daniel Brett's voice.

'It'll be in this evening's edition, and I'd like to do a follow-up, say tomorrow or Wednesday? Keep the interest going. Makes a good feature. At this time of year things get a bit dead.'

'What time of year?' she asked.

The reporter looked at her sharply.

'You really don't know?'

She shook her head.

'September, fifteenth September. Season's tailing off round here. So are newspaper sales. The holiday crowd thins down now. Well, if it's OK with you, I'll be back during the week.'

* * *

'Do I have to stay in bed?' she grumbled, when Dr Brett returned from seeing the reporter off the premises.

'You need the rest.'

'Why?' she demanded. 'I'm not ill.'

'Sleep won't do you any harm. Especially after a shock like you've had.'

'You don't know I have.'

'No,' he agreed. 'But it's a pretty good guess. Rest now anyway, and we'll see how you are this afternoon.'

'Must I?' She sighed loudly. 'I'm fed up with lying here. It's so boring.'

'There's a TV,' he suggested. 'Would you like me to switch it on?'

'OK,' she replied grudgingly.

He handed her the remote control.

'All yours,' he said, before silently disappearing once again.

* * *

She leaned back, letting her head sink into the pillows, changing channels on the television through cartoons, an old black and white film and American football until she found a bland, morning chat show.

After half an hour or so, she began to doze, losing interest in the programme. She had no idea who any of these people were, much less what they were talking about.

She was beginning to feel like someone from another planet—nothing in this world was making sense to her—not even some mid-morning programme which didn't exactly appear to be taxing on the brain.

A while later, she was aware of the lunchtime news coming on but tiredness prevented her from taking any real notice.

She was nearly asleep when a pale image of her own newly-discovered face loomed behind the newscaster, startling her, and she swiftly turned up the volume of sound.

'. . . the Cornish coast.'

It was too late. The picture faded from view and a sports report filled the space. Whatever had been said about her was gone. But what had it said, she asked herself.

Had it mentioned who she was? That she was missing? Excitement flared through her body, then drained away just as rapidly.

The picture was of a girl with straggly, fair hair, how she was now. Not a missing person. Either the police or the reporter had supplied one of the recently-taken photos. They must have used a Fax machine, she reasoned.

A Fax machine. That was something else she remembered. Her mind strained backwards trying to discover more.

Why are some things so easy to remember, when the vital ones are not, she wondered in despair?

Her head slumped into the pillow, tears seeping sideways to soak the crisp cotton. And the black mist that clouded her every thought closed in round her more deeply than before.

CHAPTER THREE

The cat rolled over on to its back, languidly raising all four paws in the air, inviting her to stroke the soft fur. But her gaze skipped to the door of the cottage, seeing its black paint peeling a little in places where the hot sun had burned into it.

She stretched out one hand to touch it. Letting her fingers push it gently, it creaked slightly as it opened and she could see the faded hues of the Persian rug against the red clay tiles of the tiny porch.

To the left, she knew, was a long, sunny lounge with french windows leading out to a red-brick patio. The sloping lawn led down to the stream.

To the right was the dining-room, low-beamed, with a dark-polished, oval table, and there were flowers brimming from jugs and vases everywhere.

Every room in the cottage was filled with flowers. Even in winter there were dried leaves, hydrangea and poppy heads, honesty, twigs of old man's beard, rose-hips or haws.

And there was the fragrance of potpourri. Rose and lavender-scented in summer; cinnamon and spice in winter. She could smell it now, a sharp, tangy spiciness.

*   *   *

'There's someone here to see you.'

Daniel Brett's voice made her open her eyes. The clear-cut planes of his face were sharp, taut, almost grim. His blue eyes for once held none of their usual humour.

She looked past him, to the man standing behind his shoulder. He was tall, taller even than Daniel.

He was broad-shouldered and deeply tanned, with a thick mane of tawny hair that reached almost to his shoulders.

When he smiled at her, his teeth were very even, their whiteness intensified by his suntan. But his eyes, she noticed, didn't reflect that smile.

'Elly! Darling!'

His mouth descended on hers, and she recoiled at the unexpected movement, unable though to avoid the lips that crushed into hers.

Instinctively her hands thrust themselves against the barrel of his chest, trying to push him away.

She heard the rumble of his laughter, felt his body vibrate under the pressure of her fingers. He moved backwards and she saw his narrowed eyes again stare into her own.

'That's not like you,' he observed.

His head turned to Dr Brett.

'Quite the opposite, in fact. Elissa isn't usually so backward about coming forward. She has such . . . passion. Isn't that true, Elly?'

She gazed at him, wide-eyed.

Was it true? He made her sound like a . . . She dismissed the word that sprang into her mind.

Who is this man, she wondered. He obviously knows me very well—and yet I have no idea who he is. I might have thought he was family until he started behaving the way he did.

Her mind was in turmoil trying to work through all the different thoughts. This was quite a shock.

'Well, Elly, get dressed. I'm taking you home.'

'That's one thing you're not doing, Mr Chivers,' Daniel Brett snapped out and she was startled by his anger.

The other man stiffened.

'And why not?'

'She's not recovered enough to go anywhere yet.'

'Recovered? From what? Loss of memory?' the man grated. 'Not exactly an illness, is it? Anyway, time will soon cure that.'

'I said, Elissa is not going anywhere.'

There was now more than a hint of steel in Daniel Brett's tone.

'If you're worried about lack of fees for keeping her here, I can soon sort that out. Money's no problem with me.'

'Money doesn't come into it. It's Elissa's health I'm concerned about, Mr Chivers.'

'But there's nothing wrong with her!'

'I'm the doctor, Mr Chivers, not you. And Elissa will be staying here until I'm perfectly satisfied she's fit and well again.' He paused, his grey-blue eyes glinting. 'And, until I know exactly what caused the state she was found in.'

'Too much sun probably,' the other man retorted. 'She was found naked, wasn't she?'

'For goodness' sake,' she shrieked. 'Will you both stop talking as though I'm not in the room!' She glowered up at the man. 'Who are you anyway?'

'Oh, come on, Elly. Don't play games with me. You know perfectly well who I am.'

'I wouldn't be asking you if I did.'

'OK then, we'll continue this little charade if we must. I'm Mark Chivers and we're engaged to be married. Satisfied now? I really don't get what you're playing at, but you must have some perfectly good reason.'

Elissa stared at him. Engaged to be married? To this man?

'I think Elissa needs to rest now, Mr Chivers.'

'Oh, do you! Well, I haven't finished talking to her yet. There's a lot I want to hear. And in private, if you don't mind.'

Daniel Brett eyed him levelly.

'I do mind. Elissa is in my care. And the last thing she needs is trouble of this kind. I think you'd better leave, Mr Chivers. Now.'

For a moment Elissa thought Mark Chivers was going to protest further. The air between the two men was electric and their antagonism a tangible force.

Then Mark swung round on his heel and strode towards the door. In the doorway he paused.

'I'll be back tomorrow, Dr Brett, early. Make sure Miss Waverley is ready to leave by then.'

* * *

After he'd gone, Daniel grinned at Elissa.

'For one moment I thought he was about to swing you over his shoulder and head for home.'

Elissa smiled ruefully.

'So did I. I was petrified.'

Daniel raised one eyebrow.

'Petrified? Surely that's not the way to feel about one's fiancé.'

Remembering Mark's earlier words about their relationship, Elissa felt a wave of colour burn into her cheeks.

Daniel began to smile.

'What are you blushing for, Miss Waverley? He certainly seemed to know you quite well—you're obviously not a stranger to him.'

'Will you please stop it!'

'Really, Miss Waverley!'

'And stop calling me Miss Waverley.'

'It's apparently your name. Elissa Waverley. Rather nice I think, don't you?' His eyes were suddenly serious. 'Does it ring any bells?'

She shook her head.

'How about Elly? Or even Lissa? I think it suits you.'

'I really think I should get some sleep now,' she announced.

His eyebrows registered surprise.

'You did say I needed rest,' she reminded him.

'You're right, I did. In that case, I'll leave

you to it.'

He drew the curtains across the window, shutting out the bright sunshine, and left her.

Elissa eased her body under the covers, letting her mind digest the morning's events.

Mark Chivers—the name meant nothing. But then, neither did Elissa Waverley.

He was good-looking in a rather arrogant way. She wondered what sort of job he had.

Running a club maybe—health and fitness. He had that kind of bronzed appearance. He appears to know me pretty well. Too well, she decided, still squirming at the way he had greeted her.

She wriggled her head into a more comfortable position on the pillow, then lifted it suddenly.

So why didn't he make any comment about my appearance? Even I know that I don't usually look this bedraggled and uncared for.

* * *

She was climbing the stairs, straight, steep, narrow stairs bordered closely by the walls.

The door ahead of her had a low lintel and she remembered she must bend her head as she went through. With thumb and finger she lifted the wrought-iron latch.

As it swung inwards, the door creaked, catching slightly on the fringe of a Persian rug covering the polished, wooden boards of the floor.

It was a bright, sunny room, the leaded windows open at each end, their flowered curtains billowing.

The four-poster bed was high, with cream lace covers and valance.

She smiled when she saw it, remembering its comfort, its warmth and she could imagine snuggling into it right now.

Like a shadow, the cat slipped past her, soft fur brushing against her bare legs.

'No, Toby,' she warned, bending to pick him up before he could jump on to the bed. 'You know you're not allowed on there.'

The cat nuzzled its head into her neck, the soft silk of its body heavy in her arms.

Her fingers ran down its back and the cat began to purr.

Through the window she could see the garden.

Its borders were full of colour and her eyes were drawn to the dovecote, although nowadays there were no doves any more.

She also noticed the wavering line of the stream as it passed under the wooden bridge and into the spinney alongside the garden.

The water looked clear and cold and she could almost smell the freshness as it babbled along.

Badgers lived there and came at dusk to eat the scraps put out on the patio for them.

There were at least seven or eight of them

now. It always surprised her just how large they were, a bit like small bears.

One of her greatest pleasures was watching the animals as they shuffled around the garden late at night.

She leaned on the windowsill, her arms still clasping the cat, rubbing her chin against his head.

She recognised the flowers that grew in the garden as the same varieties as those in the vases in the house. Whoever lived here obviously loved the garden with a passion.

There were roses just below the window, clinging to the whitewashed wall.

Red. A deep, velvety red, with a heavy scent that cloyed the air. She closed her eyes, shutting out the garden.

But the thick scent of roses still hung there, catching at her throat.

* * *

When she opened them again, morning sun glinted on the metal rail of her bed, creating a rainbow dazzle of colour.

And through it she saw a woman, looking down at her.

'Elissa, darling. Oh, your beautiful hair! It looks so thin and . . . unwashed. Whatever have they done to you?'

The voice was light, well-spoken, and yet Elissa had the impression that it held no sincerity.

It was as if the words were carefully rehearsed.

She raised her head.

'Oh, darling, please be careful.'

'I'm not ill.'

'But you're in hospital, darling. Something must be wrong.'

'It's nothing really, nothing physical anyway.' Then seeing the perplexed expression on the woman's face, she explained, 'I've lost my memory.'

'Yes, I was hearing that from Mark.'

'You know him?'

'Of course I know Mark, darling. I'm his mother.'

'Are you?' Elissa replied.

'You really have lost your memory then?'

'Do you think I would joke about something like that?' Elissa retorted sharply.

'I'm sorry, darling.'

With gloved fingers, the older woman leaned forward and patted her hand.

'Mark was quite distraught. I had to come to see you. And try to persuade that awful man . . .'

'Awful man?' Elissa interrupted her.

'Dr Brand, or whatever his name is.'

'Dr Brett.'

'Well, whoever he is, he has a most obstructive manner. Mark was furious when he got back home. There's no reason whatsoever why we can't take care of you. You're Mark's fiancée. He has every right to decide what happens to you.'

Elissa was annoyed by the woman's tone.

'No-one has any right to make decisions for me. I'm perfectly capable of doing that myself.'

'Not according to that doctor. Anyway, you can easily discharge yourself. There's no way he can stop you. I'll go and organise it.'

Elissa sat upright.

'I don't want to discharge myself.'

'Oh, don't be so silly, Elissa. Mark wants you home with him. He loves you. He needs you.'

'I'm staying here.' The words came through gritted teeth. 'And now I have to rest,' she added defensively.

Mrs Chivers' thin, lined face pouted, and Elissa noticed that her scarlet lipstick was smeared at the corners of her mouth.

'You're being ridiculous, you know, Elissa.'

'Once I know what's happening, it will be different. But for just now I need time to sort things out in my head.'

'And that's something you'll do far better in familiar surroundings with us.'

'You live nearby?'

'Really, Elissa! You really do seem to be in a muddle. Of course we do. The other side of Helston—where we've always lived.'

'A whitewashed cottage with a black door?' Elissa asked eagerly.

Mrs Chivers stared at her.

'Cottage? Of course not! Chiverton Hall could hardly be described as that.'

CHAPTER FOUR

'I do have to rest,' Elissa reminded her, desperate for the woman to go away—and leave her in peace.

'I shall have a word with that man on my way out. You can do any resting at Chiverton Hall. All he's after is a nice fat fee for keeping you here. Ridiculous! Obviously desperate for money. The place is almost deserted.'

'There are other patients then?' Elissa questioned.

'Not in this wing.'

'But there are others?'

'Oh, yes. There's an orthopaedic ward near the main entrance. Wheel-chairs and frames lined up all along the corridor. Frightful hazard. Shouldn't be allowed. There were patients coming and going there.'

Elissa gave a sigh of relief. So the place wasn't empty after all. It had just seemed as though it was because it was so quiet.

'And nursing staff?' she asked.

Mrs Chivers frowned and peered closely at her.

'Of course there are nursing staff. The place is a private hospital, isn't it? Did you hit your head on something to cause the amnesia, Elissa? I can't see any bruises.'

'No-one seems to know,' Elissa replied. 'Do you mind leaving just now—I really must sleep.'

'Well, I'll be back. So will Mark. He's had to go up to Truro today. Never tells me where, or why. Probably something to do with the patients.'

'Patients?' Elissa echoed. 'You mean the patients here?'

'Oh, really, Elissa! Do concentrate, darling. At Chiverton Hall, of course. Surely you must remember. You're the physiotherapist. The whole place is grinding to a halt without you. That's why Mark needs you back there so desperately.'

Physiotherapist. So that's what I am, Elissa thought. Well, I wouldn't be much good at the moment. I haven't a clue what to do.

Still, it does provide at least one small piece in the jigsaw about my past. I must tell Daniel. It might help.

But Daniel wasn't around. It struck Elissa as a bit odd considering he always popped up whenever someone came in to see her.

Mrs Chivers was gathering up her handbag.

'I brought you some flowers, darling. They're on the side there. But in this heat they'll need water soon, otherwise they'll start to wilt. I'll give Mark your love, shall I, as soon as he returns?'

Without waiting for her to answer, Mrs Chivers left the room, leaving a trail of exotic perfume haunting the air.

Elissa leaned back, exhausted by even such a short visit. She couldn't understand it—this tiredness washing over her all the time wasn't like her.

Or perhaps it was. If she was a physiotherapist she would have thought she would have been full of energy.

But perhaps that wasn't the case at all.

She tried to remember what physiotherapists did. Manipulating limbs . . . easing joints . . . stretching muscles. Somewhere in the back of her mind she could put together the information even though she knew she wouldn't be able to put it into practice.

'Has she gone?'

Daniel was standing in the doorway, looking apprehensive.

'Coward,' Elissa said, laughing. 'She's half your size.'

'And a million times more fierce,' he replied, with a smile that crinkled his eyes in a way that Elissa was growing to like. 'She scared me half to death.'

'Don't be so cruel! Anyway, she thinks that I ought to be at home with them.'

Daniel pulled a rueful face.

'Don't I know it! She was tearing me to shreds out there, before she came in to see you. She thinks all I'm after is the money.'

'And are you? How does this place run?' Elissa asked. 'It doesn't appear to be overcrowded.'

'In answer to your first question, no. To your second—with difficulty. And to your third—unfortunately it's half empty.'

'But why? I thought private medical care was on the up and up. People are always willing to pay for it.'

'It is a bit off the beaten track down here.'

'Surely that's an advantage. All this peace and quiet. Perfect tranquillity to rest and recuperate.'

'You've got to get here first,' Daniel observed. 'Still, it is early days.'

'How early?'

'Trevellian House opened in June.'

'And now it's September,' she said. 'Three months isn't long.'

'It is when you've Chiverton Hall operating ten miles away.'

Elissa stared at him.

'Chiverton Hall is a private hospital, too?'

'It started out as a health farm, but slowly it's been widening its horizons and it's more of a private nursing home now. With their kind of money, they can attract consultants—and patients.'

'According to Mrs Chivers, I work there,' she said.

'I'm sorry?' Daniel looked puzzled.

'Physiotherapist. So Mrs Chivers has just told me.'

'So I've been here for three months and I've never bumped into you before. I'm not usually so sloppy! I must be starting to lose my touch.'

'Can't you be serious for once?' Elissa frowned.

'What would you like me to be serious about?'

'Why weren't you here to protect me from that woman for a start?'

'I've already told you she terrified me and I was kept busy answering the phone. The police have had dozens of calls since your picture appeared in last night's paper and on the TV.'

'But I've been identified by the Chivers,' she protested.

'Then it seems you have plenty of look-alikes all over Britain and even some abroad.'

'Perhaps the Chivers have got it wrong, too,' she said, 'and I'm not Mark's fiancée. But how am I going to find out?'

'Difficult,' Daniel replied. 'But there must be some way of being absolutely certain.'

'Any ideas?' she persisted. 'All those people who've phoned could be just as sure as he is.'

She glanced down at the all-enveloping hospital gown she was wearing. 'Birthmarks or scars—any identifying marks. Isn't that what people look for?'

Daniel shook his head.

'You haven't any. I discovered that when I

was examining you.'

Elissa felt her cheeks burn at the certainty in his reply and was aware that he noticed it, too.

'It's part of my job—I'm sorry, I didn't mean to embarrass you,' he said. 'It's especially necessary when we don't know who the patient is or what's wrong with them. Sometimes it makes things a little bit easier. Now, this afternoon, I think a spell in the garden would do you good.'

'I would love to go outside.' She smiled, glad that he'd taken the initiative to change the subject.

'Good,' he replied. 'But first we'll have to find you some clothes.'

* * *

The September sunshine filtering through tall trees dappled the lawn with an ever-changing pattern of branches and leaves.

Elissa felt its warmth through the dark blue T-shirt that Daniel had lent her. A pair of his denim shorts were belted round her waist, but even so, they drooped almost to her knees.

While they strolled down a sloping path that crackled with dried leaves, she studied him through half-closed lashes.

It was no wonder his clothes hung on her. Despite his lean body, his height governed their size and length.

His face was interesting rather than handsome, she decided. His face was too long and angular; his nose not quite straight; and his chin was decidedly determined.

But his eyes made up for any imperfections—startlingly blue flecked with grey, they were very expressive.

His mouth was full and sensuous—the type she would like to kiss. She began to imagine it right there and then.

She stopped, standing stock still in the middle of the path.

Where had that thought come from? She hadn't even considered him especially attractive and now here she was imagining what it would be like to kiss him.

Daniel turned to look at her.

'Are you all right? Not feeling faint or anything are you? We'll go back if you are.'

'No, I'm fine.' She hurried to catch him up. 'Just admiring the view.'

'With your eyes shut?'

She watched his face as it broke into a smile.

'I was listening to the birds,' she added quickly.

'The wood pigeons do make a lovely sound—very soothing. Come on, it's not far now. We're almost at the beach.'

A breeze, warm on her skin, ruffled her hair. Her tongue slid over her lips and she tasted salt.

The path gave a final twist and ended in a stone wall.

Daniel pushed open a rather creaky wooden gate and held it for Elissa to go through.

Her bare feet crunched and sank deeply into the fine shingle, making every footstep an effort until she reached the wet sand. It was firm, leaving only the imprint of her toes.

Tiny waves rippled towards her and she crossed a piece of dried seaweed that prickled her heels, before stepping into the shallow water.

'Is it safe to swim?' she said.

He looked at her with amusement.

'Now? You're not really dressed for it, are you?'

'No,' she said, laughing back at him. 'I meant the currents. Lots of these little coves are quite dangerous. You can be swept out to sea in seconds if you're not careful. You have to make sure you choose your swimming times very carefully.'

'So you are a local.' His eyebrows lifted. 'Only people living round here know that sort of thing. That's why so many tourists get caught out each year and have to be rescued—if they're lucky.'

'Then I do belong at Chiverton Hall after all. Or has anyone else locally claimed me?'

'Dozens, from what the police are saying.' He glanced down at the watch on his wrist. 'We'd better get back. The phone's probably going berserk with even more.'

'Will you take me to the place on the cliff where I was found sometime?' she said, lengthening her stride to match his. Eventually she found herself running a little in order to keep up with him.

'You think it might trigger off some reaction?' he asked.

'Do you?'

'It's a possibility.'

His wide mouth pursed as he thought about what may happen.

'But considering the circumstances in which you were found, anything you do remember might be a bit of a shock. It wouldn't be good for you to get upset just now.'

'Right now, it would be a blessing to have any kind of memory—just to make me feel normal again.'

* * *

As they rounded the final bend and reached the top of the path, a babble of voices floated back to them.

'Wait here,' Daniel ordered, pushing her down on to a wooden seat under an overgrown rhododendron bush, while he strode off towards the old manor house.

Elissa did as she was told, glad to rest after climbing the slope. Daniel had reached the patio now and disappeared in through the

French windows which opened on to it.

The voices rose. It sounded like quite a crowd and she wondered what it was all about.

As she watched, the french windows opened again and a thin girl in jeans and red vest slipped out.

Instinctively, Elissa swung her legs over the back of the seat and shrank into the overgrown branches of rhododendron, letting the thick, shiny leaves close round her.

The girl was standing on the patio, looking round, shading her eyes from the sun. A camera swung from one shoulder and Elissa decided she had the look of one of those nosey reporters.

And I'm most likely to be her prey, she thought.

Parting the leaves, she could just see the patio and the girl. She inched her body closer into the dense bush. With an indignant squawk, a pigeon shot upwards in a flurry of wings. The girl swung round. Staring intently, she began to move across the lawn.

Elissa tensed, hoping she had enough strength in her legs to run farther into the trees surrounding the garden.

She began to wish she was safely back in her hospital bed with its protective metal rails.

The girl had reached the path now and stopped, her eyes searching the wooded area.

Another few yards and she can't fail to see me, Elissa thought, not daring to move again in case she disturbed any other wildlife in the bush.

Out of the corner of her eye she saw a huge brown caterpillar undulating along a leaf towards her cheek. If it reached her . . . a shiver travelled down her spine making the hairs on her arms stand on end.

Which is worse, she wondered, a nosey reporter desperate to get her hands on the latest story, or an enormous caterpillar that seems to be growing even larger the closer it comes?

She could almost feel its rippling body glide over her skin and she watched it for a while to see what it would do next.

'Come on then. I'm not happy about you wandering about out here on your own. I'd rather you were inside with the others.'

Daniel's unexpected order made Elissa jump and the stiff green leaves of the bush wavered.

The caterpillar vanished, leaving Elissa wondering where it had gone. Reluctantly, the reporter turned back, taking one more quick look around her, and followed Daniel inside.

With a sigh of relief, Elissa bent her head and emerged from the bush to settle herself on the seat again.

She could hear the drag of shingle down in the cove as the sea washed over it, and she could still smell salt in the air.

It gave her a sense of peace—until she saw

Mark Chivers striding over the lawn towards the house.

What on earth was about to happen now, she wondered. A confrontation was just about the last thing she needed.

CHAPTER FIVE

Elissa couldn't help thinking Mark Chivers was more than a little unpleasant, as she rose to her feet and started to cross the lawn.

But despite the fact he was a bit arrogant and overpowering, there was no doubting his good looks. He was also obviously wealthy, if Chiverton Hall was as successful as Daniel said.

He had everything going for him—and yet . . . Elissa couldn't quite work out why she found him so unappealing. Yet surely she must feel something for him. They were supposed to be engaged, after all.

She glanced down at her left hand but there was no ring. She looked closer. Not even a pale band left in the suntan to show where it had been.

Perhaps we haven't been engaged long enough to buy one, she reasoned. Or perhaps I'm not his fiancée at all.

It could easily be that I'm somebody entirely different. The idea shook her a little.

But his mother had seemed pretty certain. Or was she tied up in the mystery in some way, too?

Mrs Chivers had seemed very self-assured and positive about Elissa's identity. And the police appeared to be quite satisfied as well.

Elissa had reached the french windows and hesitated before going inside. The big room, which Elissa guessed was a lounge, was filled with people, all talking at once.

They continually talked over the top of each other, their voices becoming louder and louder.

Daniel stood, glowering at them, with Mark at his shoulder. Elissa remained just outside, listening intently.

'So who's this guy then?' one voice shouted above the rest.

'Me?' Mark smiled. 'I'm Elly's fiancé, Mark Chivers, owner of Chiverton Hall, over near Helston.'

His words produced a buzz of noise, everyone waving notebooks in the air to catch his attention.

Elissa groaned inwardly. More reporters. She didn't think she was worthy of causing such media interest. The situation was very strange.

'So where's your girlfriend then? We're all waiting to see her.'

'Resting,' Daniel Brett interrupted firmly. 'She's not fit enough to be interviewed.'

Mark turned back to the reporters. 'Dr Brett seems determined to keep my fiancée to himself. And I can't really blame him—that's exactly how I felt when we first got together.'

Elissa squirmed. This wasn't right. She found Mark Chivers mildly embarrassing and that wasn't how you should feel about your fiancé.

She tried to imagine being in love with him but couldn't.

Even if she had been before her memory loss, she certainly wasn't now. Elissa felt incredibly confused by the whole situation and her first instinct was to panic, but she knew that wouldn't do her any good.

'Come on, Doctor Brett, you can't keep her hidden away for ever. It's our right to see her,' someone else was calling out.

'And it's my right,' Daniel said in a tight voice, 'to protect my patient.'

'Why don't you all ask her what she thinks?' Mark threw in. 'She's out there on the patio.'

Eyes turned and, before Elissa could turn and run, the crowd surged forward, cramming themselves through the opening of the french window in an effort to be first.

But it was Mark who succeeded. His fingers reached out and gripped Elissa's elbow, dragging her forward.

At the back of the throng, white-faced with anger, she could see Daniel, trying to push through.

'Miss Waverley will answer any questions you want to ask,' Mark said with a smile of triumph. 'After all, you've nothing to hide, have you, darling?'

Furiously, Elissa tried to tug her arm free, but his hand tightened, keeping her from moving away.

She gazed back at the sea of moving faces, deafened by the cacophony of voices shouting questions, trying to grab her attention.

'What happened out there on the cliff, Elly?'

'My paper wants to do an exclusive, Miss Waverley. We're prepared to outbid any other offer.'

'We'll outbid anyone.'

'Don't sign anything, Elly, until you hear our offer. We've a helicopter waiting.'

The crowd was closing in round her, jostling. Hands stretched out, grabbing at her. Shoes trampled on her bare feet.

Terrified, she tried to step back to get out of their way, but Mark was there, preventing her.

'Any offers you'd like to make, I'll deal with,' he called out. 'I shall be acting for Miss Waverley in any transaction.'

'Will you all please leave.' Daniel's voice rang out above the rest. 'Immediately, before I send for the police.'

Elissa could see the sharp outline of his face as he joined her, his grey-blue eyes glinting like steel, his chin jutting.

The babble ceased momentarily.

'Come on,' Daniel hissed in her ear, swinging her sideways, across the patio and in through the french window. He slammed it shut behind him and turned the key.

Outside, furious faces pressed against the glass, misting it as their mouths shouted, and knuckles rapped.

Elissa felt decidedly faint and her legs began to give way. But before she hit the floor, Daniel caught her, lifting her into his arms and out of the lounge into the corridor.

She could feel the rapid thud of his heart beat against her cheek under the soft cotton of his shirt.

The slight prickle of his chin grazed her forehead but not in an unpleasant way. It made her feel safe and comfortable.

His feet moved silently over polished floors and then up the stairs.

For a moment, he stopped halfway to adjust her weight, then continued. Elissa was grateful he had been there to catch her. She let her head sink into his shoulder, comforted by his strength supporting her.

'That stupid fool!' he burst out and the words vibrated against her ear where it was pressed into his chest. 'Submitting you to an ordeal like that. He's obviously even more thoughtless than I first anticipated.'

'How did all those reporters get in here? Who told them? Did someone tip them off about me?'

He lowered her gently on to her bed, and she was reluctant to lose contact with him.

'It makes a good story—naked girl found wandering on cliff,' he growled. 'Too good to resist when the girl's lost her memory as well. There's a grapevine for this sort of thing.

'Usually what happens in cases like these is that someone relays the details to every newspaper. Basically, they're all on the look-out for a scoop, especially at this time of year when there's not a great deal happening.'

His mouth tightened into a straight line.

'I wouldn't be surprised if it was Mark Chivers himself.'

'His mother did say he'd gone to Truro.'

'That's probably it then. I was beginning to wonder how he managed to time things rather neatly, arriving when he did to act as master of ceremonies. A very clever move, even for him.'

'You don't like him, do you?' she questioned, clasping her knees to her chin as she sat on top of the bedcovers.

His mouth relaxed into a grin.

'Is it so obvious?'

'Well,' she replied, 'let's just say you could cut the atmosphere with a knife when you're together.' She looked down at the T-shirt and shorts she was wearing. 'Do you want your clothes back now?'

He began to move towards the door.

'You can hang on to them for the time

being. I'll go and phone one of the nurses. Get her to buy something for you in Helston on her way in. There's just about time before the shops close.'

Some time later, Elissa studied herself in the mirror. It wasn't quite what she would have chosen for herself, but the pale blue of the denim dress emphasised her tan. She tightened the thin leather belt and smoothed the flared skirt over her hips, turning slightly to view the back.

'It suits you.'

She felt herself blush at the note in Daniel's voice as he came through the doorway.

'You've done something to your hair, too, haven't you?'

'Only washed it,' she said casually, glad that the young nurse had thought to buy a few essentials to add to the dress, underwear, T-shirts and jeans she'd chosen. 'It was thick with sand and salt. How did you get rid of those reporters, by the way?' she asked, keen to keep their personal conversation to a minimum.

'I didn't. They're still roaming all over the grounds.'

'Don't you mind?'

'Of course I mind. But as long as they're not disturbing my patients, there's not much I can do about it, is there? I can't physically throw them out. I think that would do us a lot more harm than good.'

'What about Mark Chivers?'

'He seems to have gone home. There wasn't much he could do once you'd come back to your room.' He paused before adding, 'And if he had made any attempt to come in here . . .'

'I don't think physical violence is the answer,' Elissa said, smiling.

'But it's a tempting thought,' Daniel growled. 'And talking of tempting, I think you could do with a relaxing evening out tonight.'

'Where?' she said eagerly.

'Not too far,' he warned. 'Helford's fairly quiet and there's a good place to eat there, down by the water.'

'Helford,' she repeated.

He looked quickly at her.

'That name means something?'

She shook her head.

'But earlier you said Helston, didn't you? Where Sarah bought these clothes?'

'Two different places. Helston's quite a sizeable little market town with a lot of history, whereas Helford is much smaller—just a collection of pretty cottages and houses by an estuary.' He looked at her quizzically. 'Maybe you're not a local after all.'

She began to flick a comb through her hair.

'So when do we go?'

'How about now, ten minutes or so?'

'You don't waste any time, do you?' She smiled.

The grey-blue of his eyes darkened.

'No, Elissa,' he said quietly, 'I don't.'

The car park at Helford was on a hill, overlooking the river mouth out to the open sea. For Elissa it had been quite a nerve-racking journey.

To avoid lurking reporters, they'd set off through a back entrance from Trevellian House.

This had entailed travelling along a lower driveway full of pot-holes and overhanging bushes, until they reached an even narrower lane.

Elissa didn't like to say that Daniel was driving too fast, but every twist and turn threw her sideways, almost on to his lap.

The car, she realised, was unfortunately far too old to require seat belts and without them, the well-worn leather seat let her slide. By the time they had travelled down the final tortuous bend of a hill, she felt stiff from the effort of clinging to the doorstrap.

Daniel, she noticed, appeared to be part of the car itself, leaning into every bend as it swung round corners.

But then, of course, he did know the countryside better than she did. Perhaps if her memory came back she would know this part of the world just as well. But for the time being, there was no way of knowing.

She looked at Daniel out of the corner of her eye. His thick hair was blown into a tangle, swirling over his forehead, and his eyes were intent on the road ahead.

His long fingers held the steering-wheel lightly, his deeply tanned wrists and arms hardly moving at all as he controlled it.

Close up, she could see the dark shadow deepening his jawline and the fine lines etched around his eyes.

He wasn't what you would call classically handsome, she decided, but he was definitely attractive nonetheless.

'If you're not careful, you'll put me off my driving, looking at me like that,' he said, catching her off guard.

'What makes you think I'm looking at you?' she asked. 'I was keeping an eye on the speed—we're going far too fast you know.'

How on earth did he notice? She was trying to be as subtle as possible.

The car slowed, swung into an opening and bounced its way across a grassy slope.

'Well, you can stop panicking now. We're here.'

The view over the river-mouth was beautiful in the evening sunshine. Yachts leaned into the wind, miraculously avoiding windsurfers as they spun past, sails taut.

Others that were moored revolved slowly, and Elissa could hear the faint tap, tap of ropes against masts.

A dog barked, splashing into the shallow water near the edge, to retrieve a stick.

Every faint sound was carried to her on a

breeze that ruffled her hair.

'Come on then.' Daniel's hand lightly brushed her bare arm. 'Will you be warm enough?'

He leaned into the back of the car and grabbed a sweatshirt, slinging it over one shoulder so that the sleeves hung down to the waist.

'You can borrow this on the way back if you're cold.'

As they crossed the grass, she stumbled over a rock that jutted out from the undergrowth.

Wavering, she reached out to grab hold of Daniel's arm.

'Careful,' he said, taking her hand. 'You don't want to end up back in bed with a broken ankle, do you?'

When she looked up at him, his eyes were large and slightly heavy, their blackness leaving only a thin rim of grey-blue to reveal their true colour. She felt a shiver travel down her spine.

She could hear the waves ripple against the shore, the dog was still barking and there was the sound of the rattle of rope on mast . . . the mutter of rooks roosting in branches above, mingled with the rustle of tall, dry grasses beside her on the bank.

Her own heartbeat thudded so loudly that she was sure it could be heard far out to sea.

She was still holding his arm, and abruptly removed her hand, but she couldn't escape from the slow burn of his eyes.

And nor did she want to.

The sound of a car coming in through the entrance broke their mesmerising spell and Elissa stepped backwards, her long skirt brushing long stems of cow parsley that filled the hedge.

Neither of them spoke as they descended the hill, and at the bottom crossed a narrow wooden bridge spanning the mud where the tide had yet to return. But it wasn't an awkward silence, Elissa decided. It felt like they had said so much already.

CHAPTER SIX

Elissa hesitated in the pub doorway. Inside she could hear the hubbub of voices. It reminded her of the afternoon and the mass of reporters seething round her.

'It's OK,' Daniel murmured, moving up close beside her. 'Quite safe. There's a table over there.' He ushered her gently towards it. 'I'll find a menu.'

The sun was almost gone now, colouring the ripples on the water rose-red to merge with the yellow of the lights from inside that were reflected on the river.

She could see Daniel, head and shoulders above the others round the bar, his fair hair still ruffled.

After a moment, he began to walk back to where she was sitting. He was carrying two menus and handed her one as he sat down.

'What do you recommend?' she asked, taking the leather-covered list he offered.

'Any of the fish. It's always good, and fresh. Caught this morning usually. The crab's delicious. The salmon superb. The plaice out of this world . . . There's nothing like locally caught produce—so much better than the stuff that's had to come speeding down the motorway, prepacked and having seen better days.'

'All right! You've convinced me!' Elissa laughed, and after having a quick look down the menu, she finally decided on the plaice stuffed with crab and prawns.

'Better than the meals at Trevellian House?' Daniel asked when they were served ten minutes later.

'Would I dare to criticise?' she hedged, tucking into her meal with great relish.

It had been a long time since lunch and she was starving.

'Knowing you, yes.'

'But you don't know me,' she replied.

He shrugged slightly.

'Don't I?' he said softly, leaning across the table towards her.

'So the delicate little patient isn't resting after all. What a bit of luck.'

The unwelcome voice jarred through her,

and she raised her eyes to see Mark Chivers standing over her.

Behind him, her face bright with triumph, followed the girl reporter Elissa had seen that afternoon in the garden.

'I'm sorry, Lissa.' Daniel's face was grim. 'Shall we go?'

'I haven't finished my meal,' she said automatically.

'But . . .'

'And I certainly don't intend to run away.'

Daniel relaxed back into his chair and lifted his wine glass, a slight smile spreading across his face.

'No,' he agreed. 'You're absolutely right.'

'You don't mind if we join you, do you?'

Mark Chivers was dragging another chair towards their table.

'Yes,' Daniel said quietly. 'We do.'

'Still determined to keep her all to yourself, Doctor Brett? Now that's not fair. Not when she's my fiancée.'

'And what about the young lady with you, Mr Chivers?' Daniel enquired. 'Are you going to abandon her?'

Mark's handsome face creased into a smile.

'Of course not. She's here for an exclusive interview—and now she'll get one, won't she, Elly, darling?'

Elissa sliced into her fish, and, extracting a juicy prawn, popped it into her mouth and chewed it slowly.

'Elly? Did you hear what I said?'

Elissa picked up her glass of white wine and sipped it. When she replaced it on the table again, Daniel poured in a little more.

'Elissa!' Mark's voice had an edge to it now. 'You do realise you're acting like a silly child. This isn't going to look good when Paula here writes it up, you know.'

Elissa finished the last mouthful of fish and vegetables on her plate and laid down her cutlery.

'I think I'll have a dessert, if that's all right with you. We're not in a hurry, are we?' she said to Daniel. 'The apple pie and clotted cream sounds good, and coffee as well, thanks.'

'Not at all. If you would like dessert then it's not a problem.'

Daniel rose to his feet and went over to the bar.

'Stop playing the fool, Elly,' Mark said through gritted teeth. 'Paula is here for an interview, and she's not leaving this place until you talk to her. It won't take any effort.'

It was quite dark outside now. Only a glint here and there, reflected on ripples, showed where the water flowed.

Elissa leaned her head against the window, savouring its coolness. Reflected in the glass, she could see Mark's anger grow, and Paula jotting something in a notebook.

She was curious to know what it could be.

She wasn't aware she'd said anything even vaguely newsworthy, unless she was writing down what Elissa had just eaten for her evening meal.

'Do you want cream in your coffee?'

Daniel had returned.

Elissa nodded, reluctant to say anything, even to Daniel. She had to force herself to eat the apple pie. Every mouthful was an effort.

When the coffee came, it was far too hot to drink, and she sat gazing out of the window into the night, wishing the evening would come to a rapid end.

It had been a lovely night up until half an hour ago. The dislike between Daniel and Mark enveloped them all.

She could sense that Daniel was all ready to jump into an argument with Mark, but was being restrained for her sake.

Paula sat with a small, self-satisfied grin on her face, constantly writing. Elissa grew more and more curious about its content.

It also seemed as if she was prepared to sit there all night, just waiting for Elissa to talk.

Well, she wasn't going to. This reporter didn't have a hope of getting any type of story from her—and they were all too good at making something out of nothing.

So her only option was to sit in silence, finish her coffee and then get up to leave.

She hated spoiling Daniel's night like this—but if she wanted to keep her dignity intact she had no choice. Draining her coffee cup, Elissa smiled at Daniel and stood up.

'I think I'd like to go back now.'

* * *

Mark's car—a rather showy BMW—was far too close to the rear of Daniel's, Elissa decided, watching its headlights in the rear-view mirror.

With bends like these, all Daniel had to do was put the brakes on too sharply and the other vehicle would crash straight into them.

Surely Mark must realise the kind of danger both he and Paula could be in if he didn't slow down.

The lane reminded her of a tunnel, with its dense trees almost meeting above, and the reflection of the car lights bouncing back from them.

Elissa's fingers gripped the leather door-strap, trying to prevent herself being flung from side to side as they spun round corners at breakneck speed.

Why didn't Mark slow down? He was forcing Daniel to drive much too dangerously.

She could see the grim thrust of Daniel's chin outlined in the light from the dashboard and sensed his growing anger. But there was no way he could stop or even slow down. Mark was too close.

Unexpectedly, the little car swerved

sideways, over the grass verge and into a farm gateway, leaving the BMW to hurtle past.

Then Daniel swiftly reversed out into the lane again, and pushed his foot hard down on the accelerator.

'Daniel, don't be ridiculous,' Elissa said, realising that Daniel wanted to get his own back on Mark.

She saw the bright red glow of the car's rear lights ahead of them, growing closer and closer. Night air bit into her skin, making it sting, and she felt it tug at the thin strands of her hair, making them whirl around her head.

'Slow down, Daniel. Please.'

At that point, Daniel must have taken his foot off the accelerator and Elissa found she was able to breathe again, releasing her tight grip on the leather strap.

'Sorry, Lissa. I didn't mean to frighten you, but that man is a maniac! Driving like that, in these lanes. It's suicidal.'

'You didn't have to copy him.'

'I just wanted to give him a taste of his own medicine. He could have had us in the ditch on these bends. They're tight enough to get round, without someone clinging to your tail. I really have no idea why some people have to show off like that. I suppose the flashy car has a lot to do with it.'

He turned the steering-wheel and the car slipped down a track so narrow that it was hardly wide enough for them to get down,

Elissa thought, viewing it through the brightness of the headlights.

At least they'd slowed down considerably, even if she had no idea where they were.

She could hear the scrape of thin twigs. Some reached in to brush her face, startling her. Let's hope we don't meet anything coming the other way, she mused.

Knowing our luck right now, it would probably be a huge lorry or something, just what we need!

A damp, muddy smell caught at her nostrils and she guessed they were close to a tideless creek.

'Are you OK?' Daniel's voice was anxious.

'Fine,' she said.

'Not the best way to treat a convalescing patient, tearing round the countryside like this in the middle of the night.'

'Surely it's not that late?'

'Not far off. It's time, anyway, that all my patients were safely tucked up in bed.'

'To be honest, I'm not really that tired, although I could have done without the excitement of the journey we just had!'

'Do you remember anything about the pub—do you think you've been there before?' Daniel asked.

'I couldn't really say,' she said. 'But there was nothing about it that triggered off any memories.'

'If you lived round this way, I'm sure you

would have done. It's quite the place to go. Out of season, that is.

'In the summer months, it's packed out with tourists. The locals don't tend to bother with it too much then.'

'Maybe I'm a tourist then,' Elissa said forlornly. 'But how are we ever going to know? This is an impossible situation—when am I ever going to remember anything about my life?'

Tears of frustration pricked at her eyes.

'Don't worry,' Daniel comforted her. 'I'm sure it won't be long now.'

It was with relief that Elissa returned to her room and settled down into her bed again. Safe. Secure. She was growing to like the room. Within a few minutes she was nodding off to sleep.

* * *

Toby was sitting on the window-sill in a pool of sunshine. His attention was held by something, or someone, down in the garden and she moved over to the window to see what it could be.

Someone was hoeing the border, half-hidden behind a flowering bush, just beyond the dovecote.

She could see hands gripping the wooden handle and the ragged sleeve-edges of a fawn woollen jumper. A booted foot, embedded in moist soil, leaned towards the travelling hoe.

She smiled. Dad was so proud of his garden.

Shooing an indignant Toby to one side, she unlatched the window and opened it, putting her head through the narrow gap to call out to him.

Someone else was in the garden now. She wasn't sure who, but she could see them coming up through the copse towards the stream—a blurred figure, hazed.

Mist was rising from the thin line of water, making it difficult to make out exactly who it was, a man or woman.

A prickle of apprehension started down her spine. Dad! She had to warn Dad.

He was quite oblivious, hoeing away happily, unaware . . .

She opened her mouth. But there was no sound. Her throat strained to get the words out. She must warn Dad somehow . . .

CHAPTER SEVEN

She woke with her scream still echoing round her.

Daniel was in the room, standing over her.

'It's OK,' he soothed, holding her close as she sobbed. 'You were dreaming again.'

'Dad,' she said. 'It was something to do with Dad. He was in the garden. He didn't know.

But I did.'

Tears streamed down her cheeks and her whole body shook.

'He didn't know what?'

She shook her head helplessly.

'Something . . . Something awful was going to happen. Dad was in the garden. He loved the garden. And then . . .'

She screwed up her face in an effort to remember, but once again her mind was a total blank.

It was as if a thick brick wall had been built, separating the past from the present.

Daniel's fingers caressed the nape of her neck and she closed her eyes, savouring the sensation they created.

'Don't worry,' he said gently. 'You'll remember one day.'

'But when?' she cried. 'It's been days now and I don't remember anything.'

Daniel sat down on the side of her bed, and she noticed for the first time that the side-rails were not in place.

But she couldn't remember when they'd been removed, or who had removed them.

'It doesn't happen overnight,' he told her. 'It sometimes takes quite a while. Occasionally never at all. It all depends on exactly what happened to cause the trauma, and also on the person concerned. You may not want your memory to return, Lissa.'

'But I do, I do,' she wept.

'Maybe it's not what your mind wants. I told you before, it's a form of protection. Cutting out the bad memories or experiences completely. And it isn't really up to us to decide whether the memory should come back or not.'

His arms loosened and he rose to his feet.

'Now, do you think you can go back to sleep again? If not, I can give you something to help.'

She glared up at him.

'I'm not having any more injections or tablets.'

'It could be what you need,' he suggested.

'No!'

She lay, once he'd gone, wishing he could stay. Just his presence was comforting. It made her feel a lot more secure somehow. And yet, at first, she'd been so sure he'd been behind the whole situation.

Why ever did I doubt him, she thought.

Her thoughts turned to Mark and his insistence that they were engaged.

She had to find out whether it was true and tomorrow, she would go to Chiverton Hall to get to the bottom of it.

* * *

In the morning, Elissa realised she had no idea where Chiverton Hall was. And she had a feeling it wouldn't be all that easy to find out without people getting suspicious.

The nurse, Sarah, had brought in her breakfast tray. Daniel was, Elissa discovered by asking her, off duty.

It was a very rare occurrence.

And now that he was safely out of the way, Elissa realised she could quite safely escape for a while. But there was still the problem of how to get to Chiverton Hall.

'Do you live near Helston?' Elissa enquired, when Sarah came to collect her finished breakfast tray.

The girl smiled.

'Born and bred there.'

'Is Helston far?' Elissa asked casually.

'From here?' Sarah picked up the tray. 'Seven or eight miles, I reckon.'

'Do you come by bus?'

'No, my boyfriend is a porter here. So we always come on his motorbike.'

She moved towards the door.

'Buses don't run very often. Not when I want to come here, they don't.'

So she was still no further on in getting to Chiverton Hall, Elissa thought as she washed her face in the little basin under the mirror.

Wearing the jeans and one of the T-shirts Sarah had brought her, she wandered out into the garden. Daniel hadn't told her to stay indoors, and after yesterday's outing and the walk to the beach before, she couldn't see that there'd be any problem.

Daniel's open-topped car was parked under the trees where he'd left it the previous night.

She stood beside it, remembering the speed they had travelled along the lanes with Mark Chivers hot on their trail.

Daniel's navy sweatshirt still lay crumpled on the front seat where he'd thrown it when they returned to Trevellian House.

Instinctively, she leaned in to smooth it out, and as she picked it up, saw his car key underneath.

A thought ran through her mind—it was an open invitation. Slipping into the driver's seat, she put the key into the ignition and turned it. With a roar, the engine surged into life.

Elissa pushed her foot down on the clutch, eased in the gear and released the handbrake.

The car inched forward and she swung the wheel to avoid ending up in a flower bed.

Well, at least I know how to drive, she thought delightedly, and urged the car down the gravel drive.

At the stone gateposts, she stopped, wondering which way to go—left or right.

Taking a gamble on the situation, she decided to turn right. She hoped she'd be able to retrace her route if she'd got it wrong.

About half a mile farther on, she passed a signpost which told her Helston was eight miles away.

At least she was on the right track.

It was easy to follow the signs—right again

by Culdrose helicopter base, left down into the town.

Chiverton Hall was somewhere just beyond this point, Daniel had said. But where?

She stopped in town and asked for directions, realising she wouldn't be able to find it otherwise.

Elissa repeated the instructions she'd been given to herself as she drove. The driveway was just past a bend.

With so many it wasn't easy.

But when she saw the tall, granite pillars with very imposing wrought-iron gates, she knew she was in the right place.

The long gravel drive was immaculately kept, not a single weed growing through.

A bit different from Trevellian's pot-holes, she reflected. This was obviously a family who took great pride in their surroundings.

Each side was bordered with glossy rhododendron bushes and shaggy blue-headed hydrangeas.

When she reached the house, it was magnificent, another old Cornish manor, but quite regal.

So what do I do now, she wondered, bringing the car to a halt behind a line of shining limousines.

'Elly, darling!'

She gritted her teeth as she heard the familiar voice. Mark Chivers was crunching his way across the gravel to greet her.

'I'm so glad that you've finally seen reason and come back to us, darling. We have missed you.' The tone of his voice sent a shiver through her.

Mark's arm curved round her waist and gripped her as though she would run away if he let go.

He was guiding her up the stone steps while he spoke, and in through the ornate front door.

Inside, she paused, gazing round.

A wide wooden staircase spiralled up from the black and white tiled hall, its gleaming brass banister ending in an eagle, beak stretched, wings outspread as if to fly.

The walls were hung with huge, gilt-framed oil paintings, each one lit up separately.

Sunlight streamed in from tall, stained-glass windows either side of the entrance, patterning the white floor tiles with rainbows.

In one corner was a vast reception area, with marble-topped desk and a collection of coloured telephones.

The whole effect was of some outrageously ornate and expensive film-set and Elissa felt quite sure this type of setting could only have been designed by Mrs Chivers.

'Mother is having breakfast out on the patio,' Mark told her, turning her in the direction of a door. 'You know the way. I'll catch up with you later. Things to do.'

Assuming Elissa knew where she was going,

he strode off towards the front door again and she heard it slam behind him.

Elissa opened the door in front of her and found it led into an enormous lounge.

Several large sofas, patterned with bright flowers, were lost in it. A beautiful marble fireplace took up most of one wall and open french windows led out into the garden.

She could see the back of Mrs Chivers seated in a lounger with a table beside her.

As if sensing her presence, the older woman turned her head. She smiled widely when she saw who it was.

'Elissa, darling! What a lovely surprise. How on earth did you manage to escape that awful man? There's another chair over there. Pull it over, darling. Would you like some coffee?'

'No,' Elissa said, obediently doing as she was told. 'Thank you.'

Mrs Chivers poured coffee for herself and raised the cup to her lips.

'So how did you get here, darling? Taxi?'

'I borrowed a car.'

'Does Mark know you're here? He's only just gone out. Always here and there. Never tells me where. Of course, I'm only his mother.'

Mrs Chivers flicked open a gold case and tipped out a cigarette, then lit it. Her hand Elissa saw, shook so much that the flame of the lighter wavered to and fro, almost missing.

'He'd better let all your patients know

you're back. There's been a steady queue of disappointed patients waiting for you.'

Elissa tensed. So I do work here, she thought. It wasn't something they'd made up.

'Everyone will be so pleased to see you again,' Mrs Chivers continued, drawing deeply on her cigarette, then puffing out a thin trail of smoke. 'And so will Mark. He's missed you so much, darling.' She gave Elissa an arched smile that never quite reached her eyes.

'Is it all right if I go and see my work-room?' Elissa asked.

'Of course, darling. You know where it is, don't you?'

Mrs Chivers' sharp blue eyes challenged hers.

Elissa shook her head.

'So you haven't quite fully recovered from your amnesia yet? I'm sure someone will show you the way if you ask, darling.'

She studied the gold bracelet watch embedded in her plump wrist.

'Paula should be at reception by now.'

Pushing back her chair, Elissa stood up. Mrs Chivers caught hold of her hand and gave it a squeeze.

'We'll have lunch together out here, shall we? About one o'clock? I'll see you then.'

Elissa went back through the lounge, still dazzled by sunshine, and into the hall.

As Mrs Chivers had guessed, the receptionist was now at her desk, telephone receiver in hand, the other writing in a leather-bound book.

The name Mrs Chivers mentioned should have meant something, Elissa realised.

Paula, the reporter, and Paula, the receptionist, were the same girl.

CHAPTER EIGHT

'So you've decided on a change of career since I saw you last?' Elissa asked, looking Paula in the eye.

The other girl's rosebud mouth stayed tight.

'I'm the physiotherapist here—so they tell me,' Elissa said. 'Or do you know that already?'

'I know that already. I work here.' Paula's voice was clipped and abrupt.

' 'Ullo, Miss Waverley.'

A gruff little voice behind her made Elissa turn. Wearing a pristine white shirt, neat green waistcoat and trousers to match, stood a shiny-faced youth, hair springing sideways into tight auburn curls that gave him rather a cherubic appearance.

'It's me, Charlie Watts. Don't you remember?'

'Of course I do,' she lied. 'I'm just going to my work-room. Why don't you come with me. I've a few things to move. If that's all right,

Paula,' she added. 'I'll only keep him for a few minutes.'

Paula looked doubtful, then nodded.

'Not more than five minutes then. He's due to take round the coffees at half-past ten.'

'Lead on then, Charlie,' Elissa said, giving him a slight nudge as he hesitated.

'Right, Miss Waverley.'

At the top of the stairs, she stopped. Looking back, she could see Paula was again speaking into the telephone.

'I'd better explain, Charlie,' she said.

'You don't have to explain nothing, Miss Waverley,' he replied with a broad grin. 'I've been watching the telly and seen all about you in the papers. Right old mystery, isn't it? Can't you remember nothing?'

'Nothing at all, Charlie, and I need someone to fill me in a bit.'

The boy's eyes sparkled and his smile grew wider.

'And you'd like me to, Miss Waverley?'

'If you can.'

He straightened his shoulders.

'What d'you want to know, miss?'

'Everything about me, my job here, my relationship to Mark Chivers, the lot.'

'Well, I've only been working here six months, miss, but you was here then. Physiotherapist, that's what they calls you. Did my knee a power of good when I twisted it down on the rocks last month. Not limping a bit, am I, now? This is your room.'

He opened a door leading off the corridor and Elissa stepped inside.

It was painted in soft turquoise, walls and ceiling, with a couch in the centre, and fitted cupboards. One end was curtained off, as a changing room, she presumed.

'What about Mark Chivers?'

Charlie's mouth grimaced.

'Lord and master, he is. Don't let nobody forget it, neither. All the women think he's the bee's knees though. Lays it on a bit thick, if you ask me.'

'And I'm his fiancée?'

'Don't know about that.' The boy shrugged. 'Could be, I suppose.'

'Do you remember the day I was found? Had I been missing from here?'

Charlie looked at his watch.

'Nobody had seen you for two days. Not here anyway. Have you tried asking round where you live. Look, I'll have to go, Miss Waverley. It's gone the half hour and I'll have to get those coffees done. Talk to you later.'

Elissa caught hold of his arm.

'I don't live here?' she questioned.

'No, Miss Waverley. None of the staff do.'

He pulled his arm free and scuttled off along the corridor. She heard his feet clatter down the stairs.

So I do work here. That's all true. But I live somewhere else. Where? Maybe that's where I was for those missing two days. Is that near Housel Bay, the place where I was found?

Elissa scanned the room once more. It was immaculate.

She opened one of the cupboard doors and the shelves were piled with fluffy white towels. The next had small pillows, and a third gowns which she presumed were for patients to use. In yet another were bottles of oils and creams.

Nothing that tells me anything about myself though. Everything is still a total blank.

A wave of despair hit her and she bit back the tears that brimmed into her eyes.

So what do I do next, she asked herself.

She didn't need to answer that question. Mark Chivers appeared in the doorway behind her.

'Darling!' he said. 'Paula said I'd find you here. Ready to start work again? Things have been desperate without you.'

'How long has Paula worked here?' Elissa asked. 'I thought she was on a newspaper.'

'Freelance,' he replied smoothly, smiling at her. 'Keeps tabs on this part of Cornwall and sends stuff in to anyone she thinks would be interested.'

'And this is a useful place to work, I should imagine. Quite a clientèle?'

'We do have a few celebrities staying now and then. She often finds she's in the right place at the right time.'

He slipped his arm round her waist.

'But let's not talk about Paula. It's you I'm interested in.'

He nodded towards the window.

'I see Brett let you borrow his car.'

'Not exactly borrow,' she said.

'I'll get someone to run it back to him.'

'There's no need for that. I'm perfectly capable of driving. I drove it here.'

'But you're not going back. There's no need.'

'Oh, yes, I am.'

He swung her round to face him.

'I said there was no need. We can look after you perfectly well here. Anyway, it's not as though you're ill. Just a little memory loss, that's all. It'll soon return.'

And then what, Elissa thought. Why is Mark so keen to keep me here? Or Daniel, for that matter?

What is it that's hidden in my mind?

'Let's see what we can do to trigger it off, shall we?'

Before she could protest, Mark's mouth descended on hers. One hand slid up her back to caress the nape of her neck but Elissa began to pull away. This wasn't what she wanted.

She felt nothing for this man and she needed to get away from him. Catching him off guard, she managed to slip out of his clutches.

She ran down the stairs and out through the front door, aware of Mark calling her name behind her.

Gravel shifted under her feet as she ran to the car and fitted the key in the ignition, praying it would start first time. It did, and with the engine racing, she spun it round and back down the drive to the main road. Now for Housel Bay, she thought.

She stopped in Helston to ask the way again and realised she would have to pass the gates of Trevellian House to reach it.

About half a mile from them, the engine spluttered and died. The car had run out of petrol.

There was nothing else she could do but push it on to the grass verge and start walking.

And the only place she could walk to was Trevellian House . . .

As she rounded the final bend in the drive, Daniel came storming out to meet her.

'Where have you been? We've been going frantic searching for you. There are people down on the beach, out in the woods, everywhere. Do you realise how much trouble you've caused?'

She was amazed at his fury.

His grey-blue eyes were like steel; his face taut. His whole body radiated anger.

'And as for my car—what have you done with that? If it's in a ditch . . .'

'So that's the problem, is it?' she blazed back. 'Your precious car. Well, you don't have to worry. It's quite safe. I ran out of fuel half a mile or so down the road.'

'Where have you been, Elissa? Why didn't you tell me where you were going? I've been worried sick.'

His tone had moderated now, the tension of his body relaxing.

Elissa braced herself. She could guess his reaction to what she was about to say.

'Chiverton Hall.'

'What!' He could barely contain his surprise.

'I wanted to see the place. I decided it was time to see whether it brought back any memories.'

'And did it?' His voice was gentle as he stood, looking down at her. She realised his concern was genuine.

She shook her head.

'None at all. But at least I've proved to myself exactly who I am.'

'Chivers was right, was he? You are the physiotherapist there. I have to admit I thought he was lying.'

'I saw my work-room. And there was a boy. He knew me instantly. And that girl, Paula, the reporter, was there as well. She works as the receptionist. Apparently the reporting is just a casual thing. Freelance. She picks up stories and sells them to any newspaper she can. I gather they have quite a celebrity clientèle at Chiverton Hall, so she can probably find out a lot of information.'

Daniel put his hand on her shoulder.

'And you're feeling OK?'

'Fine. And now I want to go to Housel Bay, where I was found. You could come with me if you like.'

'No.'

'What do you mean, no?' she demanded.

'For one thing, I'll have to go to collect my car, and for another I think you've had enough for one day.'

'But there's so much to be done,' she protested.

'You've done far too much already.'

'If I go and rest now . . .' she pleaded.

'We'll see.' His eyes crinkled.

'I'm sorry about your car. But when I found the key was there . . .'

'Don't worry about it—I'd rather you got some rest,' he ordered, 'while I try and find my car. Where did you say it was?'

* * *

She could hear waves. Somewhere out there in the darkness they were pounding over rocks.

And there was spray. A fine spray that dampened her face and hair making it cling to her neck in uncomfortable strands.

She could taste salt on her lips and it was cold, too. Very cold. She shivered. Her jeans and sweatshirt were soaked.

Voices echoed, reverberating round the

cave.

Two voices, or was it three? She couldn't be sure. Her ears strained as she listened.

Someone, or something, was leaning against her. Leaning against her back. It was so heavy.

She tried to raise a hand, push them away. But her hand was caught behind her, tied.

Whoever was leaning, groaned at her movement. She tensed.

'Dad?' she whispered. 'Are you all right?'

*   *   *

'Dad!'

'It's only me. Sarah. Sorry if I woke you.'

Elissa opened her eyes, seeing the brightness of the sunshine filling her room, but the dark gloom of the cave still hung over her.

'Are you all right?' Sarah asked coming to the side of the bed. 'Dr Brett sent me to see if you were awake.'

'He's back then? He's found his car?'

'Yes, he's found his car.'

Sarah laughed.

'Worships that old thing, he does. It's his pride and joy. He seemed just as upset about losing the car as he did about losing you this morning.'

Elissa was pulling on her clothes.

'What's the time?'

'Just past two. I've brought you a tray of smoked mackerel and salad. And you have to finish it all. Oh, and that good-looking chap from Chiverton Hall was over.'

'Mark?'

'Yes, that's him. Tall, fair-haired man.'

'What did he want?'

'You, from the sound of it. Dr Brett and him had a bit of an argument out there on the lawn. Raging away, they were. I thought they were going to come to blows.'

Elissa picked up a comb and pulled it through her tousled hair.

'Is Mark still here?'

'You're supposed to be eating, Miss Waverley,' Sarah scolded.

'I will, I will.' She stabbed the fork into a shred of lettuce. 'Is he?'

'No, Dr Brett managed to get rid of him. Backed off down that drive like a bat out of hell. Now, don't you just push that round your plate like that. 'Tis good food and not to be wasted.'

Sarah stood over her until she'd finished every morsel and then put the plate back on the tray.

'There's fruit salad to follow.'

'Oh, Sarah! I'll burst if I eat any more.'

'Nourishment, that's what you need. You need to put on a little weight if you expect to get better.'

'Please, Sarah. I really have to go.'

'And where may I ask?'

'Dr Brett's taking me out for another drive.'

Sarah frowned at her.

'Again? Very favoured, you are. Never known Dr Brett to take more than half an hour away from this place before, and here you both are off again two days running.'

'Dr Brett said Sister Thomsett takes over when he's not here.'

'She don't get the chance that often. Practically married to his job, is that man.'

But not today, Elissa thought, and slipped out of the door before Sarah could say any more.

CHAPTER NINE

So where are you taking me this time, Doctor Brett, Elissa wondered as she wandered out to the grounds where she found Daniel with his car.

Daniel raised his head from where he was polishing the bonnet of his car with a yellow duster.

'Where did you go in this, Lissa? It's filthy.'

'Well, it looks clean enough to me. Can we go to Housel Bay? Please.'

'Too risky.'

'Why?' she asked.

'Look, it's only a few days since you were found out there. Your memory shows no sign of returning. I'm not going to risk too great a shock when, or if, it does.'

'If?' she echoed.

He tucked the duster into the pocket of the car door.

'I did warn you that it might never return. It all depends on exactly what happened, Lissa. If it was too traumatic . . .'

'If we don't go there, we shall never know,' she retorted.

'We will,' he said, 'in time. But not yet.'

'You can't stop me going.'

'If that's what it comes to . . .'

'You wouldn't dare!' Elissa was shocked.

'You should know better than that. Now let's call a truce, shall we?' he said, opening the car door.

'So where are we going?'

'Not far,' he said, revving the engine. 'I'm back on duty at five o'clock. I'll take you to the lighthouse on Lizard point. You get quite a view from there.'

Elissa eased her shoulders into a comfortable position on the seat, counting every pot-hole down the driveway.

Daniel noticed and pulled a rueful face.

'The hospital itself is my first priority, but mending this will have to be the next—if I ever make the place show a profit.'

'Chiverton Hall is very grand,' she said, and immediately regretted it.

'I've been making a few enquiries about that place,' Daniel replied. 'I told you it started out as a health farm, didn't I?'

Elissa nodded.

'Well, in the last few months they've been concentrating more and more on residential patients. It's all supposed to be very hush-hush, but I gather that the Chivers are attempting some miracle cure for ageing.'

'Can they do that?' Elissa asked. 'I thought things had to go through extensive testing.'

'They do. But rumour has it that the Chivers are treating their patients for a variety of ailments with acknowledged homeopathic remedies. What other substances they're using as anti-ageing agents, no-one seems to know.'

'You mean they're experimenting on patients? They can't do that.'

Daniel slowed the car at a corner, then increased the speed.

'Who's to prove it?'

'Surely someone can? People working there must know what's going on.' She was silent for a moment as a thought crossed her mind. 'I worked there. Do you suppose that's what . . .'

'Unlikely,' he said quickly. 'You were a physio. Nothing to do with the medical side.'

'Yes,' she agreed, 'but I might have stumbled on something. Maybe that's why Mark and his mother are so eager to get me back.'

'Forget it, Lissa. I shouldn't have said anything. Look, there's the lighthouse.'

*   *   *

There were dried husks of thrift, with one or two still blooming, amongst the tufty grass on the cliff.

Elissa picked one pink head and tucked it into the top of her T-shirt. The wind was strong there, right near the edge, and the turquoise surface of the sea white-flecked.

They had walked down the lane from the carpark and she'd looked in the tiny shops at novelties made from the serpentine stone surrounding them.

None of them appealed, she decided, viewing a collection of barometers in various sizes, shaped into lighthouses.

Plastic piskies and seagulls perched on small chunks of rock, waiting for a holidaymaker to take them home as souvenirs.

Elissa couldn't quite understand why anyone would want to clutter up their houses with that kind of thing.

The Lizard lighthouse glistened with whiteness, its glass dome reflecting the sun.

Inside she could smell polish and something oily. Everything gleamed from years of polishing and cleaning. Stairs led the way upwards.

Joining holidaymakers already waiting, they followed the keeper guide and began to climb the steep steps.

There wasn't a lot of room for everyone

once they reached the lamp room and surrounded it, listening to an explanation of its power, the visibility, and more.

It was warm up there with the sunshine beating in through the thick glass. Elissa's mind began to wander and she turned her gaze out to sea.

A seagull drifted past, wings motionless, its beady eyes watching her. A tanker on the horizon looked like a toy.

She could follow the outline of the coast for miles, indented with falls of rock. People sat on the grass, lazing, picnicking while a string of hikers meandered along a path, colourful rucksacks loaded.

Dotted here and there were cottages and houses, tucked into gardens riotous with colour.

Suddenly, she grabbed Daniel's arm, jostling the man standing next to him, who glowered at her.

'Look!'

All heads turned to where she was pointing and the lighthouse keeper's voice died away.

'Over there, Daniel. It's the cottage—with white walls and a black painted door.'

* * *

It was definitely the cottage.

Elissa was quite sure of that as they stood outside the gate, looking along the gravel path to the black painted door. Even from this distance, she thought, I can smell the lavender.

'The key's under that tub,' she said, and Daniel turned to gaze at her in surprise.

'But we can't just walk in.'

'I live here,' she replied, pushing open the gate.

'How can you be so sure?'

'I just am.'

They were outside the door now, and she could see the paint peeling in places where the hot sun had burned into it.

Her fingers delved under a pot of gaudy trailing petunias and retrieved a long metal key.

'Lissa, we really can't.'

She didn't answer Daniel, but put the key in the lock and turned it. The door creaked as it opened and ahead she saw the well-remembered faded hues of a Persian rug on the red clay tiles of the tiny porch. Everything was exactly the way she had seen it in her dream.

As she went to step in, there was a swirl of movement and a tortoiseshell cat slipped through her legs and was there before her.

Triumphantly, she looked up at Daniel.

'You see,' she said softly.

There was a dry, airless smell to the cottage. Fine dust lay on the polished oval table in the dining-room as they passed its open door. Flowers wilted in jugs and vases everywhere.

But Elissa could still smell the fragrance of potpourri lingering in the heat, tangy, spicy, like the fragrance she associated with Daniel. She went from room to room, remembering. The long, sunny lounge with its french windows leading out to a red-brick patio . . .

'That's where the badgers feed,' she told Daniel. 'We put out scraps at dusk. And there's the stream, with its little bridge leading down to the copse. See, over there. Badgers have lived there for centuries.'

She rested her head against the cool glass.

'Did you know that when one dies, they find it and bury it in its own sett, then seal it up? Once, when I was quite small, we found one in the lane. It had been run over. Dad buried it in the border over there. The badgers came that night, and took it away. We watched them. They went back to the copse with it. The sett was never used again.'

'You lived here with your parents?'

Elissa shook her head.

'Just Dad and me. My mother died soon after I was born. We moved here a year later. Dad brought me up.'

Her forehead puckered into a frown and she stared at Daniel with puzzled eyes.

'He's a doctor, too, at one of the hospitals in Truro. I seem to be surrounded by hospitals and doctors, don't I?'

The cat was twirling round her ankles and she bent to pick it up, nuzzling its head into her cheek.

'Are you all right?' Daniel asked, looking closely at her.

She straightened her shoulders.

'I think so,' she said. 'It's all a bit strange. Like a dream, but not a dream. I know it all so well now I'm here.'

Still cuddling the cat, she began to climb the stairs.

'Mind your head, Daniel,' she warned. 'The doorway's very low.'

With finger and thumb she lifted the wrought-iron latch and waited for the door to creak open, then she moved towards the window.

'Would you mind opening it for me. I can't while I'm holding the cat and I don't really want to put him down.'

Flowered curtains billowed as the leaded glass flew back and Elissa sat down on the cream lace cover of the four-poster bed, settling the cat on her lap. It curled itself round and began to purr.

'It's a beautiful garden,' Daniel observed, leaning on the sill.

'Can you see the dovecote? There used to be four birds. White fantails. They were so tame. I'd feed them and they'd perch on my hand.'

'What happened to them?'

'A hawk took them, one by one. I saw it catch the last one.'

She screwed up her face.

'It was horrible. I wouldn't let Dad keep any more.'

She put the cat down on the floor and came over to the window to join him. They stood shoulder to shoulder, leaning out.

'Oh, there are still some roses in bloom.'

She breathed deeply, touching a red velvety petal with her finger.

'I thought I could smell them. Aren't they gorgeous? Roses are my favourite flowers.'

She turned her head and her cheek brushed Daniel's, sending a fire of sensation scalding over her skin.

He didn't move. He didn't look at her. But she saw his knuckles whiten as he hung on to the edge of the sill and his jaw tightened.

'Dad's made this garden so lovely,' she said, trying desperately to keep her voice even. 'He spends all his spare time out there. He'll be home soon.'

There was a strange feeling tugging at her, but she couldn't define what. A feeling of apprehension. As if . . .

'I'll go and put the kettle on.'

'Elissa.'

Daniel's hand closed over hers on the sill. His eyes were wide and dark and she couldn't quite define the look.

She felt totally mesmerised by them, not knowing that her own mirrored his. For a few moments, time stood still.

'Elissa.'

Her name sounded like music in her ears, his voice was so low. She wanted to touch his cheek, his face, and draw him towards her.

Only there was no need to do that, she realised. His face was only inches away, and growing closer. Her mouth parted.

With a tremendous thud the cat leaped from the bed on to the windowsill, startling them both.

'Toby!'

The magic was gone. Daniel moved away from her and turned towards the doorway.

'I think we could do with that cup of tea,' he said.

Elissa studied the room. Everything in the cottage was tidy, but the dust puzzled her.

It was as if no-one had been there for days. But her father was a man who liked everything orderly.

Even if she wasn't here, he'd keep it clean. She went down into the kitchen to find Daniel spooning tea into a pot.

Restlessly she paced around the kitchen before she was unable to keep quiet any longer.

'There's something I don't understand about all this. Why hasn't my father tried to find me?'

CHAPTER TEN

'It's as though no-one's been here for days,' Elissa said. 'And my father should be here. He would know I was missing. He would have searched for me. Called the police.' She stared up into Daniel's eyes. 'But the police had no report of anyone missing, had they?'

'No. That's why they didn't seem very concerned about you. Someone who is found, isn't quite such an emergency.'

'But Dad would have done something,' she insisted.

'Perhaps he thought you were with Mark Chivers.'

'I hadn't thought of that.' She frowned.

'Maybe if you were engaged, you spent quite a lot of time with him.'

'I'm sure I didn't. I mean, I don't think we are engaged.' She held out her hand. 'See. There's no mark in my tan where a ring could have been.'

'Maybe you hadn't got round to buying the ring yet.'

'No, there's no way I would have let something like that go. And, anyway, this doesn't help me find my father.'

She looked at Daniel's grave face and her own paled.

'You think that's what happened, don't you?

Something terrible happened to my father. And I was there. I saw it. That's what caused the amnesia.' Her voice faltered. 'You think I did something, don't you?'

His fingers dug into her bare arm.

'No, Lissa. That's not what I think. Look, drink some tea. All this has been pretty traumatic for you. Sit down. Please.'

Automatically, she sat down, taking the mug from him, and sipped it. She drank, letting the tea warm through her chilled body. Then she stood up. 'Those dead flowers need to be thrown away.'

'Not now, Lissa.'

'Yes! I have to.'

She moved round the house in a daze, emptying vases, gathering up the wilted blooms, taking them out to the dustbin. She returned, white-faced, carrying a crumpled panama hat.

'Dad's,' she said woodenly. 'It was lying on the path, near the greenhouse. The door's wide open. He never leaves it like that. There are special louvres to regulate the heat.'

She turned it over in her hand.

'And there's blood on the brim.'

Daniel's arms were round her, drawing her close, letting her weep. 'Whatever happened, happened to Dad, not me.'

Her mind was reaching back, searching. Darkness. The sound of waves breaking. Her clothes wet, clinging to her body.

'Please, Daniel,' she sobbed. 'You must take me to the place on the cliffs where I was found. I have to work backwards from that. It's the only way now.'

*   *   *

The sun was hazy; a pale ring half-hidden behind grey strands of cloud. Elissa shivered, wishing she'd worn something warmer. They were on a narrow path that trailed close to the cliff edge, bordered by thick bushes of blackthorn.

'Is this the place?'

'Somewhere nearby. I'm not sure of the exact spot,' Daniel answered, putting his arm round her shoulder.

She closed her eyes, trying to remember, trying to return to the darkness of that night.

'Hold me tight, Daniel,' she urged. 'Don't let me go near the edge.'

The force of the wind off the sea made her sway and she felt the strength of Daniel behind her, the grip of his fingers on her shoulder.

His foot nudged hers and a pulse of fear throbbed through her. A stone rolled from the path and bounced its way over the edge. She watched it go, as if in slow motion.

'There are steps leading down.' His voice came unexpectedly, jarring.

She held on to the rail and began to descend, spray settling on her cheeks and soaking into her hair.

A thousand memories whirled round her.

The cave. There was a cave. Or was it a tunnel? An old mine shaft leading to the sea? She couldn't be sure and all she could remember was the darkness, the dampness, the body leaning against her back and the bonds that tied her hands.

Her teeth chattered and she bit into her lip to still them. There was water now, rising up, catching at her shoes.

The hem of her jeans was soaked.

A nightmare feeling surrounded her. This had all happened before. And now it was happening again.

Had Daniel been there before, she asked herself, but her mind wouldn't tell her.

She stepped sideways from the last step on to a rock, the granite hard and sharp under her shoes.

Daniel followed, his grip relaxing away from her.

Her hands touched the cliff-face beside her, slippery and wet. She began to scramble over the rocks, trying to miss every incoming wave. Her clothes were drenched now. Just like last time, she remembered. But I don't want to remember. I don't want to know.

Daniel was close behind her, his fingers reaching out, catching at her, grasping her T-shirt, then slipping away again.

There was no way she could speak. No way

she could cry out. No-one would hear in any case.

Her hand, sliding along the cliff-face, suddenly came to nothing. A void. She turned her head to look. It wasn't a large hole but big enough for her to climb through, nothing more.

Daniel caught her round the waist and lifted her until she reached the edge. Her knees scraped on loose stones and slipped.

She felt Daniel lift her again.

She was through into dank, dark, gloom. And a terrible, terrible fear surrounded her. This was where Dad was.

This was where she'd left him all those days ago. A stream of small stones clattered round her, making her jump, and then Daniel was standing beside her.

'I can't stay in here,' she sobbed. 'I can't.'

'Ssh.' Daniel's mouth was close to her ear, his lips brushing its lobe.

'I must get out.'

'Be quiet!' The force of his tone frightened her. 'Listen!'

The roar of the waves was subdued now. She could hear a steady drip, drip of water falling from the roof. And a movement. A dragging sound. It terrified her.

Her hand clung to Daniel's and he squeezed it gently.

'Stand quite still and don't move from here.'

He released his hand, finger by finger, and

she stayed, too frightened even to breathe.

There was the faint crunch of stones, a splash as he stepped into a pool. Then silence.

Blood drummed in her ears. Her heartbeat thundered.

She could hear Daniel's voice, speaking softly, but not to her. And then another spoke, in short sentences.

'Dad!' she cried, moving forward.

'Stay where you are, Lissa!' Daniel shouted the order, bringing her to a halt. 'Go back out and fetch help. Quickly. But for goodness' sake, be careful.'

'But . . .'

'Do as you're told for once, Lissa.' He sighed wearily.

It was just as it had been before.

Scrambling through that tiny hole, lowering herself on to the rocks, feeling the sea swirl and drag at her body.

Her hand reached the rusty metal rail of the steps, hauling herself up them, her legs scarcely able to hold her.

At the top she began to run, blackthorn catching at the legs of her jeans, tearing them.

She could hear voices coming closer, hear the tramp of boots. And then a party of hikers came down the path towards her.

'Please,' she gasped, and collapsed in a heap at their feet.

Anxious faces surrounded her, eager to offer her their assistance.

‘What’s up, lass?’ someone asked.

‘Help. You must get help. The cave. Down there.’

‘Is someone trapped?

‘Or hurt?’

The voices mingled and were confused. Elissa could hardly make any sense of them.

‘Don’t you worry, lass. Couldn’t have picked better. Training exercise, this is. We’re from Culdrose Air Sea Rescue over near Helston.’

Everything was floating round her now . . . voices . . . orders . . . people moving. All she wanted to do was sleep.

Something warm was wrapped around her.

She buried her face into a shoulder, but there was no spicy smell. It worried her.

And she wondered whether it was five o’clock yet. Daniel had to be back on duty at the hospital by then.

*   *   *

The metal rails were round her again. It was as if time had taken a step backwards.

Elissa tried to sit up and her body ached.

‘Well, at least you’ve had a good sleep,’ Daniel said, smiling at her. ‘Feeling better?’

‘Dad,’ she said. ‘How’s Dad?’

His fingers lightly brushed across her mouth.

‘Don’t worry so. He’ll be OK. Tough man, your father. All that exercise out in the garden has seen to that. We've stitched up his head wound and once he's got some food inside him, he'll soon recover.'

'It's a shaft, you know. Part of an old mine. And from what I can remember, it comes out by the sea. Mark took us in from the other end. Those tunnels run for miles.'

His hand smoothed over her forehead leaving a trail of pleasure. She wanted him to stay and never leave her again.

'I know, Lissa. Your father's been telling me all about it. I've informed the police.'

'They'll never catch Mark. He's far too devious. How could he do such a thing?'

'Greed? The money was good.'

'Do you think we should let Paula have the story? She's going to be out of a job now. It would be quite a scoop, if she sent it in quickly. Could you phone her?'

Daniel grinned.

'No need, she's been here for half an hour, waiting for you to wake up. Shall I bring her in now?'

Elissa nodded and Daniel left the room, to return seconds later with Paula!

'Promise you won't sell this story to anyone else?' she asked Elissa.

'Promise,' Elissa agreed. 'You must be a good reporter. Are you all as tough as you make out?'

'It's a cut-throat business,' Paula said. 'You saw what it was like that day we all descended on this place.'

She placed a tiny tape recorder on the table.

'Now, tell me what happened.'

'No notebook?' Elissa asked.

'I can't write shorthand. Now, just when you're ready.'

'Well, I worked at Chiverton Hall as a physiotherapist, as you already know. Mark Chivers and his mother own and run it. But once Daniel Brett opened Trevellian House as a private hospital, they were worried some of their patients would change over. They needed to keep them.'

Paula leaned forward.

'So they branched out into cosmetic surgery and this anti-ageing project.'

'How did you know that?'

'Don't forget I've been working there for quite a while now. And I am a reporter, trained to ferret out interesting facts. That boy, Charlie Watts, gets around the place and he's quite a little chatterbox. So how does your father fit into all this?'

Elissa sat up higher in her bed.

'They've been carrying out research into anti-ageing at the hospital where Dad is a doctor and he became involved about five years ago.'

She stuffed a pillow behind her back.

'I don't know how the Chivers found out, but Mark was always travelling around, so they probably heard it on the grapevine somewhere. It's difficult to keep anything secret nowadays.'

'He probably heard it from you when you went to work there,' Paula suggested.

'He certainly did not,' Elissa retorted. 'I'd never talk about my father's work. He goes over ideas with me sometimes, but I wouldn't dream of telling anyone else.'

'But you must have discussed personal things with your fiancé?'

'Mark Chivers was not my fiancé. I admit he did question me about my father and what he did, but all I told him was that Dad was a doctor. Nothing more. Other people Dad worked with may not have been so discreet.'

'Not if they were women,' Paula said. 'Mark can twist them round his little finger.'

'So I can imagine. Anyway, Mark and his mother invited Dad and me to dinner one evening. It turned out that they were offering Dad a job.'

'But he didn't take it?'

'No, he turned it down flat. Mark wasn't pleased. It was quite obvious that what he wanted was to buy Dad's knowledge. Dad isn't stupid and said so.'

'From what I've seen of Mark, he doesn't give up easily.'

'He didn't. Next day he started on me, trying to get me to persuade Dad. I didn't want to know. When I came to leave that evening, I discovered my car had a puncture. In hindsight, that was suspicious. Anyway, Mark offered to drive me home.'

'And he started getting a bit too friendly?' Paula said.

'You could say that,' Elissa replied. 'Maybe he thought if he could win me over, I'd work on Dad. Anyway, I told him exactly what I thought of him. He asked if he could come in for a drink. Well, it was a blazing hot day, and he had driven me back, so I agreed.'

'What about your father? Was he around, too?'

'Dad came home shortly after and went out to water his greenhouse. He always did at that time of day. I had a drink with Mark, and it's quite obvious to me now that he'd tampered with it in some way.'

'Drugged you?'

'Precisely. Next thing I knew I was tied up down in that old shaft, with Dad bleeding all over me. Mark had hit him over the head outside in the garden. We would stay there, he told us, until Dad passed on all his information about this new research. If he didn't, then I was in trouble.'

'And were these idle threats, do you think?' Paula asked.

'Typical of Mark. If he'd thought carefully, he'd have realised that Dad and I would tell everyone what happened once we were free again.'

'If you ever were allowed to be free. He

could have left you both there. Who'd have known?'

An icy shiver travelled down Elissa's spine.

'That hadn't occurred to me,' she said. 'Surely Mark wouldn't have done such a thing?'

'He was desperate,' Paula observed. 'Desperate people do desperate things. How did you escape?'

Elissa shuddered, remembering.

'Mark thumped Dad quite a bit. I could hear him doing it. Then he tied us together. I couldn't escape with Dad unconscious. Only I could feel all this warm blood trickling over me. I've found out since that Dad's nose was bleeding, but I didn't know that at the time and imagined the worst. I had to do something.'

She paused and swallowed hard.

'Go on.'

'I was still wearing a linen jacket. Something I always wear to work. It looks smart with trousers or a skirt. The rope was tied over that, round my wrists. I eventually managed to wriggle my arms out of the jacket and the rope stayed with it. Then I climbed through the hole in the cliff face and found myself out on the rocks.'

'That must have been scary.'

'Horrible! When I saw the state I was in—blood everywhere—I just went berserk, ripping off everything I had on. I was hysterical by then.'

'And that's how they found you on the cliff-path.'

Paula switched off the tape machine and rose to her feet.

'Thanks. With any luck I'll have that in the morning edition of at least four tabloids, and maybe a couple of the broadsheets. It might even encourage one of them to take me on permanently. Maybe I'll see you around sometime.'

'Don't ever become like that, will you, Lissa?' Daniel said, getting up from a chair in the corner of the room where he'd been sitting, listening.

'She was a bit unemotional, wasn't she?'

'Not to mention ruthless!' he said, sitting down on the edge of the bed beside her.

'Can I discharge myself now? I think all my problems are better now,' she said, smiling into his eyes.

He looked startled.

'I suppose you should really. I can't keep you as a patient.'

'Good!' she said. 'So if I'm not your patient any more, then . . .'

'I'm allowed to kiss you,' he said, leaning towards her.

Pulling away gently, Elissa gazed into his face.

'I can't begin to tell you how glad I am my memory's come back.'

She leaned towards him and smiled.

'I don't want to forget this moment for as long as I live.'